Slaughter Gang

Willie Slaughter

**Lock Down Publications and Ca$h
Presents**
Slaughter Gang
A Novel by *Willie Slaughter*

Willie Slaughter

Lock Down Publications
P.O. Box 870494
Mesquite, Tx 75187

Visit our website @
www.lockdownpublications.com

Copyright 2019 Slaughter Gang

First Edition July 2019
Printed in the United States of America

Lock Down Publications
Like our page on Facebook: Lock Down Publications @
www.facebook.com/lockdownpublications.ldp
Cover design and layout by: **Dynasty Cover Me**
Book interior design by: **Shawn Walker**
Edited by: **Jill Alicea**

Stay Connected with Us!

Text **LOCKDOWN** to 22828 to stay up-to-date with new releases, sneak peaks, contests and more…

Thank you.

Willie Slaughter

Submission Guideline.

Submit the first three chapters of your completed manuscript to ldpsubmissions@gmail.com, subject line: Your book's title. The manuscript must be in a .doc file and sent as an attachment. Document should be in Times New Roman, double spaced and in size 12 font. Also, provide your synopsis and full contact information. If sending multiple submissions, they must each be in a separate email.

Have a story but no way to send it electronically? You can still submit to LDP/Ca$h Presents. Send in the first three chapters, written or typed, of your completed manuscript to:

LDP: Submissions Dept
Po Box 870494
Mesquite, Tx 75187

DO NOT send original manuscript. Must be a duplicate.

Provide your synopsis and a cover letter containing your full contact information.

Thanks for considering LDP and Ca$h Presents.

Dedication

I dedicate this book to, first and foremost, The Creator. Secondly, to my father, Big Willie Williams, for being my inspiration throughout life, who forced me into being the strong black man I am today. And to the Slaughter family: my mother, Ruby Slaughter, brothers, Christopher Slaughter, Derrick Slaughter, and Dexter Slaughter, and my two sisters and children. You all have been the motivation that pushed me to succeed. Thank you.

Willie Slaughter

Slaughter Gang

Prologue

"Damn, Teddy! What's good, bro? Long time no see," said Lil Will.

At 5'8", 190 pounds, with light brown skin and thick wavy hair, Teddy was Lil Will's little brother. He was a natural born hustler and didn't mind getting his hands dirty if it came to it. He'd been holding his brother down while he was in.

"I know, my nigga," Teddy responded. "If your ass would have stayed in Albany instead of going back to Boston, you wouldn't have had to worry about that. Anyway, how long you did on that bid?"

Lil Will had gone upstate on some trumped-up charges for possession of a firearm that linked back to a murder he had no knowledge of and a nice little trunk load of some uncut coke.

"Fifteen in, and thirty-five on paper," Lil Will replied.

Teddy shook his head in disbelief. "Damn, Lil Will, that's fucked up. You went down for some shit you ain't even do."

"Well, bro, when you a G," Lil Will shot back, "shit like that happens on a regular. But fuck all that. How's the fam? Anybody know I'm here?"

"Nah, nigga," Teddy answered. "Besides, I know you don't feel like fucking with niggas who didn't even think to send you shit or check on your family while you were gone."

"Good, and you just said some real shit. A nigga don't have time to be fucking with niggas or bitches who wasn't fucking with my campaign when I was bidding."

Teddy rolled up a whole dub of gas in one blunt. "My nigga, I'm just glad to see you out. So, what's on the agenda? I know you ready to get back to getting this real cake."

Lil Will nodded. "You know it. Best believe it's time for The Slaughter Boyz to take the streets back over," Lil Will stated. "It's hard to believe Dink let shit get this far out of hand."

Dink was their oldest brother. Lil Will had left him in

9

charge of things while he was upstate. As far as he could tell and from what his brother and other confidential informants had told him, he'd been doing some major fucking up.

Teddy hunched his shoulders and said, "Well, that's a fucking mystery story concerning that nigga."

Lil Will nodded his head before speaking on the matter. "In due time, we'll know what's happening. Until then, first thing first. Ain't a swinging dick or bleeding pussy gon' take from us what Pops built, so fuck what the streets are saying 'bout them S.M.F. niggas."

S.M.F. was the Southside Mafia Family. Since Lil Will had been gone and Dink had been running the street business, everything had gone sour. The S.M.F. had taken over the streets of Albany, Georgia with the weight at a lower price and a steady flow. Teddy had to give them their props.

"Yeah, them fools got their weight up since you been gone. From what I see, they really got shit on lock," he replied.

"Damn, my nigga," Lil Will said offensively, "sound like you a li'l scared or on some mo' shit, Teddy. I got a crew coming down in three days. It's gon' be a lot of bodies dropping if niggas ain't getting down with what we putting down."

Lil Will's choice of words hyped Teddy right on up. "Word," he replied. "You know I'm with the movement. It's Slaughter Boyz for life."

Chapter One

Bee and Ya-Ya had made their way over to the trap house. Bee was Lil Will's youngest brother. He was nineteen, 5'9", 173 pounds, with dark skin and a fresh schoolboy cut. Bee, just like the rest of the brothers, was a great hustler. He was book smart as hell. It was hard for Lil Will to understand why he didn't pursue his scholarship as a mathematician. But, then again, he was a Slaughter, and Slaughters stayed true to the hustle mentality.

At six foot even, with dreads and light-skinned and about two hundred pounds solid, Ya-Ya was Bee's player partner and street smarts handle man. They'd met right after Lil Will had gotten popped and sent upstate at Club Legion. As usual, there was a shootout and Bee was caught in the middle of heavy artillery fire. Ya-Ya had seen the li'l nigga down bad and came to his aid. When all was said and done that night, the only person with bodies to claim from busting their guns was Ya-Ya.

They sat around with Lil Will and Teddy, blazing half a pound of some Red Hair Sess and sipping on some Paul Mason on ice. Lil Will couldn't help but smile and think of all the shit he'd been missing. "Man, yawl niggas don't know how much a nigga been missing this shit."

Bee raised his glass up, showing he understood where his brother was coming from. Then he said, "Fam, a nigga been missing doing this shit with you. Did you get the packages I gave that bitch Sandy who worked there to bring to you? It should've been enough to hold you over."

Lil Will thought back to when the correctional officer had walked into his cell and dropped off the pack. She even sucked him off and gave him the pussy on the house. When she told him who it was from, he couldn't do anything other than laugh. He and Sandy end up having a good run, making money out the ass, and he tapped her sexy tall red ass every chance he got.

"Hell yeah, Bee, Lil Will replied, "Good looking out on that li'l bit."

"No pressure, big bruh," Bee responded before hitting the blunt, letting the smoke flow slowly from his mouth and inhaling it through his nose.

While they were talking, Sopia walked in followed by Kerria. Lil Will stopped talking and damn near dropped his glass of Paul Mason on the rocks. "Damn! Is that Sopia?" he exclaimed.

Teddy and Ya-Ya laughed.

"Nigga, you act like you ain't never seen the bitch before," said Ya-Ya.

"Nigga, please," Lil Will retorted, "I've seen so many bad bitches it's hard to keep up with who is who." Lil Will stood up and hugged Ya-Ya.

"Bruh, it's been a long time," Ya-Ya said.

"I know, my nigga," Lil Will replied. "Big bro home now. What's really good? How you been holding up?"

"Same ole shit, Lil Will. Killing and fucking something good. What's up for tonight?" asked Ya-Ya.

"Shit really," Lil Will answered.

Ya-Ya took a sip of his drink before saying, "Let's go somewhere fly and politick."

"Why not?" asked Bee, overhearing the conversation. He had stepped back in from the kitchen, where he was whipping up some work. "I know just the stop. Willie Bush joint uptown. We can lay low and discuss business there."

Lil Will hit the blunt three times and passed it to Teddy and said, "I'm down. Let's do it. Get everybody on the line, Bee."

"No doubt," Bee said while taking out his phone.

Sopia walked back in to the living room and plopped down on the couch next to Lil Will, who she knew had all eyes on her physique, and asked. "Damn, nigga, a bitch can't get a hug or something extra?"

"That's on me, Red Ass. Bring that soft ass here so I can

squeeze on you," Lil Will said while hitting the blunt again.

Red Ass was a name he'd given Sopia years back. Since then, while he was in the pen, he'd heard stories about her. Seeing her sexy red ass in the flesh made the stories a reality, and he was ready to be that nigga to slide between her thighs. Hugging her and taking in the fresh scent of her soft body made his dick rise to the occasion, rock hard, causing her to smile at the bulge she felt on her thigh.

Sopia laughed and said, "Nice to know I still got that touch."

They made eye contact, and the look said everything that needed to be understood. Tonight would belong to them.

Bee, Ya-Ya, Teddy, and some more of his partners had excused themselves over to the next room. They were making calls to make sure everybody was on point about the meeting that was to go down.

Bee was on the phone with one of his runners. "Listen, my nigga," said Bee, all hyped up. "We lettin' all them niggas have it that brought heat to us. Let it be known that Lil Will touched down and we are having a meeting at Willie Bush's spot tonight. Spread the word so bro can see what we're working with. A'ight, my nigga. One."

Right when Bee got off the phone, Mike came through the door and yelled at Lil Will and dapped him up. "What's up, my guy?"

Mike was Lil Will's right-hand man, a known killer. He was 5'6", caramel-complexioned, and stocky. Mike had served in the military as a Marine before some shit went sideways about a snuggling operation he and his platoon got caught up in, which led to him getting a dishonorable discharge.

After Uncle Sam kicked him out, Mike moved back to Albany, Georgia, where he met back up with Lil Will. Unemployed, but having the skills Lil Will needed in the streets, Mike was offered a job as his gunner.

Lil Will grabbed him and pulled him into a hug and said,

"You, my nigga. How you been, fam?"

Mike patted him on the back and replied, "Much better seeing you. Damn, it's been forever!" Mike looked around. "Where my homie Bee at?" he asked.

Bee stepped back into the living room. When Mike saw him, he pounded his chest twice before saying, "What up, Bee?"

Bee strolled up on him and gave him dap. "Shit, my nigga," he replied.

Mike sat down on the couch across from where Lil Will and Sopia sat all close up on each other. Lil Will realized he had something he wanted to say, but wasn't comfortable talking around Sepia, so Lil Will told her to excuse herself. When she got up to walk off, he slapped her on her soft ass, making it jiggle. *Damn, I got to hit that soon*, he thought to himself.

After Sepia was outside of earshot, Mike relaxed and spoke. "Check game. So I went to the Legion, and guess who I seen?"

"Who, that nigga Meat?" asked Lil Will. He passed Mike a Garcia Vega blunt and a half zip of Loud.

"Yeah. The nigga got nine lives or else he's a ghost," Mike replied while twisting up.

Lil Will sipped on the Paul Mason. "Well, if what you're saying is facts, them C.M.E. niggas better be on point," he said.

"Tell me about it, G," Mike said before firing up the blunt.

Smoking that gas and the oil in his cup had Lil Will's mind gone. The news he'd received in under twenty-four hours told him an underlining story. It was going to be hard trying to make money with all the extra bullshit they had to deal with.

Chapter Two

Lil Will, Teddy, Mike, Bee, and Yo-Yo fell off in the club dope boy fresh. Everybody was rocking Hugo Boss wear from head to toe. Lil Will took in the scene around him. The air was filled with the aroma of good green, alcohol, and perfume. And to top it off, ass and titties attached to bad-ass bitches were everywhere, bouncing around to the music.

"Shit!" Lil Will exclaimed.

Bee patted him high on the shoulder and yelled, "I told you this spot be lit, fam!"

"Yeah, I see Bush got it poppin'," Lil Will yelled back over the loud music. "This nigga getting that fetti! We might need to push up on some real G biz, shit!"

"Fo' sho'," Bee replied!

Mike, always on point, spotted the rest of the crew standing near the VIP sections. It was Lil Tony, Baby G, Sideway Rick, Lil Donna, Red, Mack Simp, Dogg, and their major runners and gunners.

Mike pointed in their direction and yelled, "There's the rest of the fam! Let's go!"

They made their way through the dimly lit club. Bitches shaking their asses everywhere, bottle tops popping, and different aromas of some good green set the scenery. All of it brought a smile to Lil Will's face, which diminished as soon as they were all inside the room.

"Everybody take a seat," Lil Will demanded. "Get comfortable. I'm back, and the bullshit stops now. It's M.O.B. and nothing else. Am I making myself clear?"

"Fo' sho', my nigga," Dogg replied being gone off the drink.

Lil Will raised his glass of Patron, saluting Dogg. Although Dogg was from C.M.E., the nigga's heart was big. He was one of those niggas in the hood who didn't pick and choose his battles. You bring it, he obliged. Lil Will had met him through Teddy back before he got canned. They'd become good business partners.

Lil Will lowered his glass and took a swig before saying, "We got to take the streets back. Everybody in here knows The Slaughter Boyz M.O. We answer to no one, and everybody buys our product. Feel me?"

Everybody nodded.

"Good. We take the West first. Then the East. If niggas ain't tryin' to get down, then we lay their ass down for eternity. If anybody in here ain't with it, now's the time to push on. Nigga ain't tolerating disloyalty. Period."

Nobody moved a muscle. Teddy grunted to get Lil Will's attention, who quickly acknowledged him. "What's up, Teddy?" asked Lil Will.

"What about Dink?" Teddy asked.

"Shit…"

As Lil Will was about to comment, Dink came strolling through the door with his wife and his bodyguard. Lil Will pounded him up and spoke to his wife, who was something worth looking at and marrying. *Just not that nigga*, Lil Will thought to himself as he said, "What's good, Dink?"

Dink, as egotistical as ever, responded, saying, "Not shit. I see you got everybody here. Let's talk."

"That's wassup," Lil Will said, annoyed by his oldest brother's never-ending fucked-up attitude. "Glad to have you here and on the team."

"Slow your roll, Will," Dink said offensively. "I came here because I wanted to see my brother. It's been a while, and if you didn't know, I got my own shit."

"Dink, we're Slaughter Boyz," Lil Will retorted. "No matter what, we gonna take back what's ours. Believe that."

"I feel you, my brother," Dink said, filled with laughter. "You always was that nigga."

Bee frowned and spoke up, saying, "Hold the fuck up.

Dink, what this poppin' off at the mouth shit 'bout? Where this shit coming from? Don't play. Straight talk me, fam."

Dink clapped his hands together three times and responded to Bee, saying, "This shit is ABC, Bee. Lil Will always thought he was the king of the streets. Fuck that back-stage role. I'm that nigga now, and I'm - "

Lil Will started laughing. Dink looked at him and asked, "What's so funny, Lil Will?"

"You, nigga," Lil Will shot back, "and that 'I'm the new king of the streets' bullshit-ass speech! Fool, the streets ain't got no king. Besides, I always looked up to you and wanted to be like you." Lil Will stood up and downed the rest of the Patron in his glass before speaking. "Do you want to tell the family why I really did the bid? Nigga, I caught a bid 'cause you left the gun in my car. I never said shit; never asked you for shit either."

Hearing that sparked Mike's curiosity. He couldn't hold it in. He had to know if what he was thinking Lil Will was talking about was the same as what his thoughts were. "Wait a minute," Mike said in a harsh tone of voice. "You saying Dink set you up, Lil Will?"

Lil Will waved the question off. "Don't ask me shit." He pointed at Dink. "There the nigga go."

Mike stared Dink in the eyes. Dink, feeling the pressure, defended himself by saying, "I told him Earl put it in the car, and I forgot to get it before he left."

"Whatever, nigga," Lil Will said with a smirk on his face while pouring another glass of Patron and turning it up.

Dink's facial expression went sour. He shook his head and said, "That's exactly why we can't be in the same room."

Lil Will continued to laugh and said, "Look, Dink, here's how it is. Either you're in, or you're out. You're family, so ain't no hard feelings."

"I'm out, my nigga," Dink said in defiance of his brother. "Let's go, baby."

His wife, Whitney, got up, and they left.

Teddy inhaled and choked on the chronic smoke. "Man, fuck that nigga," he said as he coughed and passed Mike the blunt.

Mike looked at Lil Will nonchalantly and asked, "Do I need to make that nigga obsolete?"

"No!" Lil Will exclaimed louder than he wanted to. "What the fuck is wrong with you niggas? It's Slaughter Boyz 'til death! That nigga will always be a Slaughter Boy!"

"You right, my nigga," Mike said. "Calm your nerves."

"However," Lil Will started saying while puffing on the blunt of Gas, "if push comes to shove, shit happens. 'Til then, let's see how he plays his hand."

Chapter Three

Lil Will pulled up to Sopia's crib, hopped out, and knocked on the door.

"Who is it?" Sopia yelled from somewhere in the house.

"Bitch, stop playing and open the door!" he yelled back, beating on the front door.

The door swung open, and so did his mouth. Lil Will's eyes roamed the full length of the sexuality before him. The mental picture he had of her from fifteen years ago was shattered by the figure standing in the doorway.

"Dammit, man," Sopia said, realizing he was stuck in the moment, "are you comin' in or what?" She turned around and walked off, leaving the front door wide open.

She didn't have to invite him in twice. He walked on in, closing and locking the door behind him. He strolled into the living room, where she sat smoking a blunt of some good and eyeing him as he walked in and sat down.

"Nigga, you empty handed," she asked. "Where the alcohol?"

"What?" he asked comically. "When did you get on the oil?"

"Nigga, it's a lot you don't know 'bout me," she said proudly, "or about what I do."

"Like what," Lil Will asked.

Sopia laughed. "Nigga, count the years. I'm a grown-ass woman. I have my own shit."

"Sounds like the same shit everybody's saying," Lil Will said with a little bit of sarcasm. "I guess you think your shit don't stink either."

"Don't put words in my mouth that don't belong to my mind, Mister," she shot back with a lot more sarcasm.

"Shhh..." Lil Will said while sliding close up on her and kissing her. He sucked on her bottom lip just to make sure she

19

knew what his intention was. The softness and taste of her lips didn't disappoint him in any way. "Damn, Sopia," he said lustfully, "you taste so damn sweet."

She smiled and said, "Boy, if you only knew. I'm sweet all over, between and inside."

Lil Will slid his hand between her thighs and started rubbing on her. "Oh, really?"

"It's only one way to find out," she said seductively, moving his hand before standing up. "You don't have to take my word for it." She stripped down to her birthday suit and threw the matching black bra and thong on the floor. "Lil Will, do you know how long I've waited for this dick?" she asked.

"Ain't no way yo' sexy ass gon' tell me or make me believe niggas haven't been tryin' to slang dick yo' way."

"What?" Sopia said defensively. "Nigga, this pussy ain't on display for every nigga to run up in. For the record, only two niggas been between these thighs, and I'm 'bout to fuck one of them now."

Right then, he pulled her close. The lust building within him for her was real. She made him feel like no woman ever did.

"Now are you gonna please this pussy or just stare at it, daddy?" she asked as she sat on the couch next to him?

"You know I'm down, girl," was his response before he started kissing her lips and then he made his way south, where he spread her legs wide and held them. Without giving it a second thought, he thrust his tongue deep inside her sex, which immediately became wet with sweet, strawberry-tasting juices. She moaned uncontrollably and became wetter and wetter as he tongued her pussy down with French kisses, sucking on the clit, causing her to cum.

"Ooooh…shit…baby…baby… That's it… That's my spot! Goddamn! That tongue is heaven sent! Don't stop! Eat this pussy, baby!" she screamed.

"Mmm… Is this pussy mine?" he asked while still tonguing

her pussy down.

"Hell yeah, baby," she proclaimed. "It's all yours! Ooooh!"

Sopia's body trembled from the explosive climax. Lil Will, with a job well done, came up for air. Without hesitation, he thrust three fingers inside of her, finger fucking her slowly, and said, "Damn, this pussy is so hot and wet."

"Uh huh... Oh baby... Yes, daddy," she said in between moans.

She reached between her thighs and rubbed her clit while he continued to stroke her with his fingers. Another orgasm claimed her body, driving her crazy. Moaning out of control, she sucked and licked her sweet-tasting juices off his and her fingers, something she knew turned him on.

"Baby, I need that dick in my life," Sopia said lustfully. "Don't play with this pussy, baby. Fill me up with that big dick."

As he entered her, she spread her legs wider. When he was balls deep inside the pussy, she wrapped her legs around his waist and locked on to him.

"Yes...baby...Fuck me! Mmm... Mmm!" she screamed at the top of her lungs!

"Damn, Sopia, this pussy good! You know you got the bomb," he said in response to her demands.

Still screaming at the top of her lungs, she said, "It's yours, baby! It's all yours! Damn, this dick is touching my soul!"

Feeling his release coming, Lil Will let it be known that he was about to cum. "I can't hold on much longer, baby! This pussy too good! I'm 'bout to cum!"

"Cum in this good pussy, daddy!" she screamed. "Cum for mommy!"

Their bodies slapped hard against each other. The sight of her hard nipples and pretty red titties bouncing around freely did the trick. Each thrust came harder and faster until the release came fast and strong, causing them to grind it on out slowly.

Feeling more than satisfied, he stood up and pulled up his boxers and pants. "Sopia, fuckin' with you, a nigga gon' catch a case 'bout this pussy."

"Why thank you for the compliment," she replied while sitting up straight. "That dick is Grade-A itself."

Lil Will chuckled and responded to her comment, saying, "Pleasure's all mine."

She left the room and went into the kitchen. Sopia was just as experienced in that field as she was at being sexy and handling her business between the sheets.

"Damn, nigga," she said, "you dicked a bitch down so good I might not be able to get up for work."

****

It was 4:30 a.m. Mike had dropped Henry off a package.

"What's good, Henry?" Mike asked, handing him the package.

"Grinding, my nigga. Some shit don't change for some of us out here. We like alligators in the swamp. A nigga come up to eat when it's necessary, and it's necessary every day," Henry said.

Henry was a kingpin in Albany, a nigga about his business. Everybody who ever crossed him or thought about crossing him ended up on a missing person's report. The nigga himself was a tall, skinny, lanky nigga. However, his paper made up for the weight he didn't have.

"Mike, I hear yo' boy Bee's brother back in town," said Henry.

"Yeah," responded Mike.

"That fool been missing in action for a minute. I hope he don't think shit still the same."

Mike looked at him sideways. "Damn, bro. What's on your mental?" he asked Henry.

"I'm just sayin', Mike," Henry said nonchalantly. "The north is mines, and ain't no bitch in my blood."

"Henry, stop tripping, my nigga. We know how you get down," Mike said.

"So you say," Henry said with a light touch of sarcasm.

"Shit ain't cutthroat like that, Henry. Lil Will just tryin' to bring more money and business into his fold. The Slaughter Boyz got to eat," Mike said.

"Shit, I'm down with the movement, Mike. Hit me on the hip and let me know something," Henry said.

"Fo' sho'," Mike replied.

Henry reached inside the driver's side of the car window and dapped Mike up. "One, my nigga."

As soon as he drove off, Mike hit Bee on speed dial. Bee's phone vibrated, and he answered.

"What's good, fam?"

"Cooling," said Mike.

"Gotta be more than cooling. Nigga, it's too early in the a.m.," Bee retorted. "Talk to me."

"Just left Henry's spot," Mike said.

"Word?" Bee said, sounding interested in what Mike had to say.

"Yeah," Mike responded, "and he knows Lil Will is back."

"Damn. News travels fast. So, what he talking 'bout?" Bee asked.

"My nigga," Mike shot back, "I ain't Inspector Gadget. But for the most part, the nigga had his questions. After I gave him some understanding, he said he was Brandy. A wary thought's in my mind, so I suggest we stay on point."

"Fo' sho', fam. Keep bird eyes on that nigga," Bee cautioned.

"I'm on it," Mike said before hanging up.

Willie Slaughter

Chapter Four

Teddy was riding through the projects on the South, collecting dues. He pulled up at the trap run by Tae, who was a distant relative of his on his mother's side. He wasn't a Slaughter, but he was still family and he knew how to hustle.

"Tae, what's good?" Teddy asked. "Why you let these niggas draw heat with all this bitchin' like hoes? You know, bruh home, and certain shit ain't flying with, 'round, or by him. Y'all niggas better get it together."

"Don't trip," Tae said. "I'm handling shit properly, Teddy."

"Alright, my nigga. Come on with the money. A nigga got shit do," Teddy said demandingly.

Tae ducked off in the crib and returned carrying a brown paper bag that he handed to Teddy. "Here you go, fam. It's an extra thirty G's plus in there for the re-up."

"Say that ain't real," Teddy said approvingly. "You been getting it in."

Tae responded, saying, "Slaughter Boyz. It's what we do."

****

Sopia sat in her apartment, chilling, smoking a blunt to the head when her phone rang. She looked at the caller ID. It was her home girl Sabrina. She answered it. "Hello?"

Always on the hype, Sabrina responded, saying, "Hey Sopia. It's me, Sabrina. What's up?"

Sopia hit the blunt before responding. "Girl, you know that nigga Lil Will back, and he ain't takin' no shorts from nobody."

"You know it's all 'bout that cheddar with niggas like that," Sabrina said sarcastically. "It ain't no secret you been

25

fucked up over him since middle school."

Sopia got a little defensive. "So what, bitch?"

"I'm just saying, homegirl," Sabrina said in a mild tone of voice, trying to smooth things over, "you been gone over the dick since way back when. Besides, your happy go-getting ass ain't been 'round since the nigga got back."

Sopia choked on the smoke. "Can't argue that. Don't worry. I'm back on my shit. He's gone back to Boston for some shit."

"Well, bitch, that's yo' freedom ticket," Sabrina said loudly over the phone.

"I know, right?" Sopia said in between coughs. "I heard Monica having something at her spot tonight. Be ready by ten."

"Say no more. Bye," Sabrina said and then hung up.

Sopia hung up and made her way downstairs in her apartment to grab something to drink. Before heading back upstairs, she looked out the window, seeing that same kind of truck Lil Will drove pass by. At least she thought she did, anyway. She shook her head in disbelief and went straight to the shower. *Damn, I gotta shake this nigga from my mind*, she thought to herself while showering.

****

Back in Boston, Mark and Lil Will were kicking it in one of Mark's spot on 13th Street.

"These pills gon' fuck Albany up. Fam, they ain't ready fo' the shit we bringing," Lil Will said enthusiastically.

"You definitely right about that, Will," Mark responded, "but, fuck 'em. Them crooked-ass pigs been getting their weight up fo' years. My nigga, we playing catch up."

Mark was Lil Will's ride and die partner. They'd met in the feds on the yard. Some fools from Jersey had tried to get at Lil Will and would've banged him up if Mark had not been there.

The two of them, along with some of Mark's homies from Boston, showed their asses on the yard that day, having the Jersey niggas airlifted for medical treatment. Being side by side in the hole, Lil Will and Mark had several conversations about getting out and getting to the paper, and here they were making their talk reality.

"That's real nigga shit," Lil Will said, hyped up.

"Let's go enjoy ourselves, fam. No need of makin' money if you can't enjoy it," responded Mark.

****

"Man, look at all these bad bitches!" Fred took in his surroundings with a smile that said "I'm in pussy heaven!" His partner Rimp had his eyes on one piece in the puzzle.

Fred was a runner. At 6'3", 222 pounds with a blue black complexion, he was about his business. He and his player partner Rimp, who was 5'8", 190 pounds with a high yellow complexion, were two of the most loyal runners in the game. Both of them worked for Lil Will.

"Yo, who's that with Lisa?" he asked Fred.

Fred looked over in the direction Rimp was pointing. "That's Tonya."

Rimp looked himself over, making sure he had his shit together. "I got to see what's on her mind."

"Fam, she fuck with Tae when he came up here once," Fred said. "Ever since then, that nigga keep more eyes on that bitch than homeland security got cameras."

"Word," Rimp said, looking surprised.

****

Lil Will and Mark found themselves sitting in the VIP section. Lil Will scoped the scene. It was a fly place with top notch females from different backgrounds.

"My nigga, you couldn't have chosen a better spot," Lil Will said, seeing two bad broads sashaying by their booth.

Mark laughed as they touched glasses of Patron. "Real niggas get served real nigga shit," he said before downing the shot.

Lil Will thought he was tripping when he saw two familiar faces in the club. "Say, fam. Ain't that Fred and Rimp?"

Mark looked up. "Damn, sho' is."

"Send somebody to get them niggas and get some more drinks over here," said Lil Will.

"I got it, fam," Mark replied.

Mark strolled out of the booth. Not two minutes later, Lil Will's phone started vibrating. He answered. "Speak, nigga."

"We got a problem," the voice on the other line said.

"What it is?" asked Lil Will

"Mike-Mike just got knocked," answered the man on the other end.

"When? With what," Lil Will asked, sounding a little paranoid.

"Hell if I know, but the alphabet boys was there," the man replied.

Lil Will rubbed the back of his head. "Fuck. Send somebody to clean house, and tell everybody it's a blackout."

"Got you, fam. One," the caller hung up.

Lil Will hung up just as Mark returned with Fred and Rimp. Mark took one look at him and could tell some shit just went sour. "What's the deal?" he asked Lil Will.

Lil Will pounded his fist against the table. "Fuck! Fuck! Fuck! Call everybody and tell them to meet up on 2nd and 3rd Street. Blackout."

Mark poured himself another shot of Patron and asked, "Damn. Is it that bad, fam?"

"Yeah," answered Lil Will, still rubbing his head. "Fred and Rimp, y'all go get Black-Eye."

"You sho'?" asked Fred.

Black-Eye was not what you would consider the average nigga. His military background, plus his Black Panther Party background, equaled a walking and talking killer. Everybody who hung around Black-Eye knew that anytime the police came through and he was around, they had to get somewhere unless they wanted to be witness to a possible cop killing.

Lil Will looked at Fred coldly. "Just do it and meet us at the warehouse."

"Got you, fam," Fred said before he and Rimp left the booth.

****

Teddy had called Bee after hearing about the shit that had gone down. "What's good, Bee? Where you at?"

"I'm on the East. What's up?" Bee asked his brother.

"Need to see you ASAP," he replied.

"A'ight." Bee looked at the time on his Citizen timepiece. "Meet me at Big-Dad's in ten minutes."

"Say no more. One." Teddy hung up.

Dink twirled around in the chair, smiling, and asked, "Where he at?"

Teddy checked his text messages before putting his phone down on the table and answering his big brother. "On the East."

Dink grabbed his car keys and jumped up out of the chair. "Okay. Let's go."

When Dink and Teddy pulled up, they saw Bee talking to a bitch named Niki. She wasn't a dime piece, but she was a good look for a side piece. Dink pulled right beside them and rolled down the window. "Yo, Bee, you slipping. Get in. Now."

Bee looked at Dink and nodded before giving Niki his attention again. "Hit my line, girl, and we'll get up on a room and do a li'l something-something."

"Okay, boo." She kissed him on the neck before he hopped in the car with Dink and Teddy. "What's up with y'all niggas?" Bee asked, lounging in the backseat.

Dink eyed him through the rearview mirror. "The question is, what's up with you, my nigga? You been off the grid. Not answering yo' phone. What's up?"

Bee smirked. "Damn, bro," he said to Dink, "we keepin' tabs now? I'm doin' what everybody else is doin'. Me."

Dink continued to look at his youngest brother through the rearview mirror. "Well, while you been out doin' you, some-body shot yo' shit up. Yo' girl down bad in the hospital."

Bee sat up straight before leaning on the back of Teddy's seat. "Teddy, this nigga got jokes or a jones in his bones?"

Teddy shook his head with a serious facial expression. "Bee, my nigga, do it sound or look like a nigga playing?"

"Shit," Bee said nervous. "How's she doing? Is she okay?"

"Far as I know, she is," answered Teddy. "Ma is going to check on her. Who do you think did it?"

"Fuck if I know," Bee said angrily, "but when I find out, the muthafucka dead." As they rode, Bee's phone went off. "Talk to me."

A man's voice came through the phone from the other line. "It's Rodney. Need to see you. Got somebody you and yo' brothers would love to meet."

It sounded like business to Bee. He perked up and pushed the personal shit to the side and dealt with the caller. "Where?"

"Spot on Corn Street," Rodney said.

"A'ight. Be there in an hour," Bee told him before he hung up. He looked in Dink's eyes through the mirror and said, "Corn Street, my nigga."

"Got you," Dink said and switched lanes.

Chapter Five

Sopia had picked up Sabrina and they were at the party. Sopia was already buzzed from the bud she'd smoked on the way there. She was feeling the vibe.

"Girl, this bitch spot is off the chain!" Sabrina yelled over the music. Sabrina was dressed in a black spandex cat suit and wearing heels to set it off.

"Monica got it jumpin'!" Sopia yelled back to her.

Sopia, herself, was putting on. Dressed in an all-black Polo body dress that stopped right above her knees and heels, she was a dime piece at the party. The body dress was fitting and hugging every curve, and there wasn't a nigga and some bitches there who weren't checking her out.

They grooved to the music and watched the door swing open. A crew of niggas dressed to impress came striding through. The one out front started yelling. "Oh shit! Looks like that whole South in this bitch! It's gon' be a fight before the end of the night!"

Sopia looked at Sabrina, who was getting amped by the minute. Seeing the expression on her homegirl's face, Sabrina yelled, "What, Sopia?"

"Brina, bitch, you know I'm ready for whatever," Sopia said, riding Sabrina's hype.

The crew they'd seen pulled up on them. Sabrina took the limelight. "What's up, niggas? I'm Sabrina and this my girl Sopia! She down!"

The young player up front laughed as he responded to Sabrina's invitation. "That's the business! We'll get up before the night is over!"

They went on their way, leaving Sopia and Sabrina dancing. As Sabrina dropped it low, twerking to "Whistle While You Twerk", the door swung open, and in walked the Slaughter Boyz with Lil Will leading the crew. Sabrina stopped in midstride and grabbed Sopia by the arm. "Oh shit! Hide!"

Sopia looked at her, confused. "For what?!"

"Yo' nigga here!" Sabrina yelled. "I thought you said he was in Boston!"

Still confused about what was going on, Sopia frowned. "What?"

"Bitch, the Slaughter Boyz are here! Look!" Sabrina turned her homegirl's face in the direction of the door. Immediately, her eyes met Lil Will's.

"Dammit," Sopia said, irritated. "Come on!"

They walked over to where Lil Will and his crew stood taking in the scene. Sopia kissed him on the lips lustfully. "Hey boo. When did you get back to Albany?" she asked.

He didn't answer. However, he turned his attention to her friend. "Who you got here with you?"

"My homegirl Sabrina," she said.

"That's what's up. Have fun. I'll catch up with you before the party is over," Lil Will said.

"Okay, boo," a dreamy-eyed Sopia said.

Lil Will and his entourage strolled on in, making small talk with some of the people as they moved through the crowd. Sabrina spotted someone and pulled Sopia to the side, breaking her out of La-La land. "Damn, bitch. Snap out of it," she told Sopia playfully.

Still in a partial dream state, Sopia said, "I'm good. What's up?"

"Ain't that Kay? This bitch got nerves showing up anywhere I'm at," Sabrina said angrily.

Sopia looked over near the front door. "Yeah, that's the bitch, but fuck her. Let's enjoy ourselves."

"You right," Sabrina said before getting back into her groove.

Sabrina screamed at the top of her lungs, "I'm gonna get some good dick tonight!"

Everybody in earshot laughed and kept partying. Sabrina was in rare form on the dance floor. She noticed a slim, tall brother watching her from the bar.

"Who's that nigga over there?" Sabrina asked Sopia while pointing in his direction.

Sopia looked. "Girl, that's Henry."

"Damn. What's he 'bout?" Sabrina asked curiously.

"That work from what I hear on the North," answered Sopia.

"That's what's up. 'Cause a bitch needs both in her life," Sabrina said, watching as he moved from the bar to stand in a corner out of the limelight.

Henry was standing off in a corner observing the scene when his eyes locked in on Sabrina and Sopia. He turned to Mike. "Who's that?"

Mike looked at her, uninterested. "That would be Sabrina, my nigga."

"Don't that bitch Sopia be with Kerria?" Henry asked Mike.

"Yup," Mike said before sipping on his Miller's Genuine Draft.

"And them hoes down with the Slaughter Boyz Right," asked Henry?

"Yup," Mike said before looking at Henry out of the corner of his left eye. "You fiendin' over the bitch or something?"

"What, nigga?" Henry said, feeling offended. "Don't play with me."

"What you saying, my nigga?" Mike shot back.

"Whatever you think, my nigga," Henry said sarcastically. "Play pussy and get fucked!"

Just as the blows were about to start, Sabrina and Sopia walked up. Sopia spoke to them both. "Henry. Mike. What's up?"

"Damn, Sopia. What's good, sexy?" asked Henry as he gave her a hug.

Mike just spoke politely.

She could tell by their body language shit was about to get

real. "It looked like y'all two niggas was 'bout to hit."

"Nothing serious. Just some nigga shit," Henry said in a cool manner. "Ain't that right, Mike?" Mike nodded in agreement.

While they were talking, Kerria approached the scene, tipsy as hell. She gave Sopia a hug. "Hey girl!"

"What you doing on the South, Kerria?" Sopia asked.

"Nah, bitch. What you doing out without letting a bitch know?" she shot back.

Sopia laughed. "Sabrina talked a bitch out of the cage. Said I'm in need of therapy to get the nigga Lil Will off my mind."

Kerria laughed so hard that it hurt her stomach. "They say that fresh out of prison dick will do that to you."

Kerria was the down for anything bitch from the hood. She was the type that if you were in a bind and needed a spot to lay low for a while, you just had to check in and pay your dues. She wasn't bad-looking either. At 5'9" and boot black, she was curvy in all the right places.

Henry saw the girls were on their girlie shit, and said, "Yo, Sopia, I'm 'bout to bounce. You girls need anything, holla at me."

Sopia gave him a hug. "We'll keep you in mind, Henry."

Before Henry could leave the scene, Sabrina pushed up on him strong. "As a matter of fact. What's up with you, Henry?" Sabrina looked at him devilishly. Henry was 6'2", 189 pounds with brown eyes.

He said, "You, li'l mama."

"Check," Sabrina said, feeling like she'd accomplished her goal. "Let me holla at you for a minute."

As they walked off, Mike shook his head in distaste. "Sopia, I don't like that nigga," he said with disgust.

Sopia saw where this was going. "Mike, chill. Henry's good money."

"Yeah, I hear ya, but something ain't right with him," Mike said.

34

Right after watching Henry and Sabrina emerge and exchange numbers, he got up and bailed without saying anything.

Sabrina sashayed back over to where Sopia sat. "What's up with Mike?"

Sopia shook her head. "Being Mike."

Henry was feeling himself. He couldn't get his mind off of Sabrina – well, off her lips, tongue, and hot and wet mouth. Her head game was super official and now he was ready to see what the pussy was hitting like.

He was prepared to free up some time and extend some currency to do it. He strolled through the parking lot over to his 7-50 Benz.

Caught up in his thoughts, he didn't realize he was slipping. Mike was already on him with the AK-47 on display, yelling, "Fuck nigga, if you ever try me like that again, I'm gon' decorate the scene with yo' ass!"

People who were outside ran back in, which caused Sopia and Sabrina to run outside to see what was up. When Sabrina saw what was going down, she got mad. "Bitch, you seeing this shit? What the fuck that nigga got going on?

"Being Mike," said Sopia, trying to figure out the best way to deaden the situation. "Dammit, man." Sopia hightailed her red ass over to Mike. "What in the hell is goin' on?'

Mike kept the AK leveled on Henry. "Just having a li'l friendly conversation. That's all. Ain't that right, my nigga?"

"Yeah, Sopia," Henry said, looking serious, "ain't shit poppin'."

Mike stepped close up on Henry so no one could hear him. "My nigga, don't let the looks trick you out of yo' life."

Henry started taking off his jewelry. "Say, my nigga, I'm a fucking man about mines. You want to hit?"

Mike looked at Henry and laughed. "What? Do I want to hit? Nigga, I love shooting fades. Let's hit."

Mike put the AK down, and without warning, he caught Henry in the jaw with a right cross. It didn't knock him out, but it damn sure dazed him.

Henry shook it off. "That's what's up, my nigga."

They went at it. The street got live and loud real quick. Everybody gathered around to see the fight. Henry and Mike stood toe to toe, trading blows.

Sopia and Sabrina decided to break up the fight. Sopia grabbed Mike, and Sabrina grabbed Henry. Both men were breathing hard and their faces was bruised.

Mike wiped the blood from his lip. "Nigga, we can do this every day."

Henry spit the blood from his mouth. "Fuck every day, nigga. We can keep going right now."

Mike tried to break loose from Sopia. She turned him around to face her. "Mike, you need to let that shit go. I know y'all niggas are bigger than this shit."

He walked off. Sabrina shook her head in disbelief. She noticed the look in Henry's eyes. "Henry, you good?"

"I'm Gucci. But that nigga a walking corpse," Henry said before he hopped in the Benz.

"Can I ride?" asked Sabrina.

He reached across to the passenger side door and opened it. "Jump in."

They drove off.

Sopia found Kerria standing near the front door. "Is Lil Will still inside?"

Kerria shook her head. "Nah. Those niggas been fled the scene. Why? What's up, Sopia?"

Sopia pulled her phone out. "Fuck! I got to call Bee. I know this shit ain't over by a long shot."

"You might be right. 'Cause I know Henry ain't gon' let that shit slide. The fucked up part is, Mike knows Henry and Bee fuck with each other the long way," explained Kerria.

"I see where you comin' from," Sopia said. "What's Sabrina dick craving ass up to?"

"Exactly that. Sucking and fucking for pleasure while tryin

to get a check," Sopia said with a smirk.

"I ain't mad at her," Kerria said girlishly.

They laughed while walking back inside, where the party was still jumping.

****

Teddy had called Bee.

"What's up, bro?" asked Bee.

"Shit, my nigga," Teddy replied. "Just letting you know them people ready to set up shop. Remember, ain't no emotion in this shit, bro. We 'bout to get this money."

"Fo' sho', my nigga," Bee said, feeling better knowing what was up. "Slaughter Boyz or nothin'."

"Facts," Teddy agreed. Where you at now?"

"A nigga in Washington taking care of some shit for bro," Bee said.

"Who, Will?" Teddy asked.

"Yeah. He's in Boston handling business. Well, he just flew back out this morning anyway," Bee said, remembering they'd crashed Monica's party last night.

"Okay, good. I'll go get them niggas and show them around," Teddy said.

"Bet," Bee said. "I'll drop tomorrow. One." As he hung up, Bee smiled. Teddy was doing the same thing.

"Damn! It's happening! We 'bout to get this money! Now, who the fuck is this that keeps blowing my line up?" Teddy answered the phone. "Yo. Talk."

"Damn, nigga," said the man on the line, "I'm calling to tell you we got a big problem."

"What now?" asked Teddy, feeling irritated because he wasn't the one for having problems.

"That nigga Mike pulled the K on Henry," the caller said.

Teddy set up straight in the recliner chair. "You shootin'

the shit, ain't ya?"

"No lie, and them niggas hit like two red nose pits," the man replied. "And you know Henry ain't gon' let that go."

That much Teddy knew was true. He pounded his fist on the arm of the chair. "Fuck! Not now! Where these niggas at?"

The man responded, saying, "Henry somewhere with Sabrina fucking like it's going out of style. Like the pussy just that good. Don't know where Mike's crazy ass disappeared to."

"Appreciate the intel," Teddy said while still thinking of a plan to stop the shit Mike and Henry had going on. "Let me see if I can get Henry on the line. A nigga ain't got time fo' the bullshit. We got that power play in motion."

"For real?" the caller replied.

"Yeah," Teddy answered. "Them niggas down here now. That's why we don't need this shit on our plate. Meet me in an hour at the Sand-Trap."

"Got you," the man on the other end of the line said before hanging up.

****

The party was over, and everybody was taking their drunk and high asses home - or as Monica had put it, "You ain't got to go home, but yo' ass leaving this bitch!" Only people left were her and the nigga everybody thought was gone or headed back to Boston: Lil Will

"Girl, what's good with you?" Lil Will asked Monica.

"Ain't shit. Why?" she replied moodily. "What's on your agenda?"

Lil Will looked surprised. "Damn, li'l mama, why you so emotional?"

"Why you actin' like you so concerned?" she shot back.

Lil Will sighed. He was making an attempt to make things

right with Monica, who was by far one of the baddest chocolate women in Albany, Georgia. Possibly in the whole state. At 5'2", 138 pounds with long hair/don't care, she was properly proportioned without children. "Look. A nigga been handlin' a lot of business lately."

"So I hear," Monica responded nonchalantly. "What brings yo' ass over here tonight?"

"A lot of shit," Lil Will said while rubbing his head. "Just getting out, clearing my mind, and tryin' to get shit moving in a new direction."

"Without me?" she said sarcastically. "Because it sho' look that way. Care to explain?"

"No. Do you," he said with a hint of annoyance.

Monica looked at him sideways. "For what?" Monica crossed her arms.

Lil Will felt guilty as hell. "Come give me a hug and let's talk about it," he said calmly.

That, he realized, made matters worse. Monica snapped. "Nigga, you got me fucked up for one of those hoes that's dick crazy!"

"Listen, Monica," Lil Will got on the defensive side, "let's have a nice conversation. Okay?"

She looked at him and took a deep breath. "Nigga, you make me sick." She walked up on him, allowing him to hug her.

"You know you my lady," he said in a soft tone of voice. "A nigga got so much shit goin' on that a nigga had to be with family for a minute. We need this move, baby. Just work with me and I promise you, we will have all the time in the world."

"I hope we're moving back to Bean Town," she snapped.

"Okay," Lil Will responded quickly, not wanting to hype her up any more than she already was.

"Lil Will, you just know I'm crazy 'bout your ass," Monica said.

"Likewise," was his comment. "But I also know I'm gon'

make this a night you'll never forget."

****

"Henry, this Teddy. Where you at, fam?"

"With Sabrina, enjoying myself. Why?"

"Meet me at The Sand-Trap in an hour. Call the S.M.F. niggas. That package just dropped."

"Got you. Say no more."

They hung up. Teddy sat in deep thought. "Now, I just got to think of how I'm gon' keep these two niggas from hitting or killing each other tonight."

Richard Boy couldn't keep from laughing. But he knew Teddy was right.

"Word. But aye, when my nigga Lil Will coming back to Albany?" he asked Teddy. "I can't believe my nigga been gone so long and he came and left without letting a nigga know."

"Shit, he popped up on me," Teddy said. "Let's handle this move. Stick close by 'cause he's supposed to hit me later on."

"Word," Richard Boy said, smiling.

Richard Boy was a Slaughter Boy to the heart. Hustling, killing, and fucking something good was all his resume consisted of. If you were family and wanted a nigga missing, you called Richard Boy. At 6'6" and 245 pounds, he was a hard hitter, but a gentle giant to the ladies.

They pulled up and around back at The Sand-Trap. Everybody who got the call was already there waiting. Teddy and Richard-Boy hopped out all business in their mannerism. Once they'd shown face, everybody else started getting out of their rides.

Henry was there with killers from S.M.F. Mike and his crew of killers was there too. Teddy could see the heat rising just like he could feel it. He let out a sigh, which was more like a silent prayer.

"What's good?" Teddy asked, addressing everyone. "Bee had other pressing issues, so he told me to step in on his behalf."

Everybody nodded, really ready to get the business over with. Henry looked across the way at Mike. Teddy didn't hesitate to grab him pulling him close, telling him, "Not now, my nigga. Let's handle this business tonight."

Still sizing Mike up, Henry smiled. "You know a nigga ain't gon' fuck up a great thing, Teddy. However, you can't save the nigga. His ass going to die."

Teddy shook his head in disbelief. "What happened, Henry? Y'all fools got fucked up and couldn't cope?"

"Nah," Henry said. "The nigga got beside himself after I asked 'bout a bitch. As I was leaving the party, the nigga upped the K on me from behind. Nigga should have handled his business 'cause now his ass gon' get cashed in."

"Dammit, man," Teddy said nervously. "A'ight. Let's just get through the night."

"Bet, fam," Henry said as he dapped Teddy up.

As they all were headed through the back-door, Teddy hit the connect to let them know they were on the way up. He knocked on the door, and a dark-skinned guy opened it. Nobody walked in but Teddy, Henry, and Mike, who quickly noticed all nine of the men who were already in the room. Teddy shook hands with them and asked, "So, y'all my fam, people?"

"That's right," said the connect, who was not a small nigga at all. He stood 6'4" and was built like a linebacker. "Let's get down to business."

Teddy and one of the men who went by the name Lee left the others, and walked into the next room, where boxes were stacked six feet high in a row. Teddy rubbed his hands together and asked Lee, "Damn, is this the work?"

"Yeah," Lee replied with a chuckle.

"Fuck!" Teddy exclaimed. "This town ain't ready for this shit."

Teddy was all smiles, but Lee maintained a straight face. "Well, what was you expecting?"

"You right, my nigga," Teddy said. "Let's get this shit up out of here. I got a team outside that's gon' move it."

"A'ight, bro," Lee said, unconcerned with how they were going to move the product.

"Don't worry. We going to show you around and get y'all up top niggas some of this southern pussy," Teddy said with a smile.

Lee hunched his shoulders, not really caring one way or another. "Sounds good to me."

"Good. Let's go," Teddy replied enthusiastically.

Lee, Teddy, and the rest of the connect crew along with Mike and Henry sat and passed around four blunts of kush while watching Teddy's, Mike's, and Henry's main runners and gunners move the shipment out of the building and into the trunks of their rides.

The whole time, Henry was on edge, really wanting to pop off on Mike for the stunt he'd pulled. But due to his word to Teddy, he decided to go with the flow until he could catch Mike's ass in uncharted territory.

****

Monica had given in to Lil Will's desires. She was lying in bed on her back, getting served some good head.

"Damn, Monica, this pussy tastes so fuckin' good," Lil Will proclaimed, face deep between her thighs.

"Yes…yes!" Monica screamed. "Eat this pussy, daddy. It's yours. Ah fuck!"

He was sucking on her clit so hard you would've thought he was trying to put a hickey on the pussy. The more she grinded on his face, the more he felt like the pussy was talking to him.

"I'm cummin', daddy," she screamed. "Ooooh…oh… baby…" He sucked on her pussy harder. "Cum on this tongue, baby."

And she did. He flipped her over and entered her from the back doggy style. She tried to prop up on her hands, but he held the arch in her back while long dicking her nice and slow.

"Ah… Monica," he groaned from the sensational feeling of her hot and wet pussy.

"Yes, baby?" she asked in a seductive voice.

"This pussy too good," was Lil Will's response.

"Yeah! Yeah! Yeah!" she screamed as he began to pound away hard and fast.

He couldn't stay up in it much longer. She met his thrust pound for pound. Her pussy was ocean wet and volcano hot. The sound of it mixed with his thighs slapping hard against her amazing fat ass was a perfect combination. They gave each other a hundred ten percent of their sex. Out of breath and well pleased, they finally collapsed on the bed. She rolled over and laid her head on his chest.

"Baby, why don't you just get out the game and be with me?" she asked him.

"Monica, we been over this," Lil Will replied. "I will be soon. I'm just trying to make sure we're good and my mama straight. Trust me. I'm getting out."

"Good," Monica said, feeling pressure removed by his answer. "The sooner, the better."

They went to sleep holding each other.

Willie Slaughter

Chapter Six

"Good morning, baby," Monica said, walking through the bedroom door. "Rise and shine. I got you breakfast in bed."

Lil Will sat up in the bed with a smile on his face. "That's why you my number one," he said.

She smiled devilishly and said, "You going to take me shopping today?"

"Girl, I would love to," Lil Will said, trying to sound reassuring, "but I got to go handle this business with the fam. Do you want to come? We can take you shopping after the fact."

"Shit no," Monica said quickly. "Ain't nobody wearing shit bitches dressing in down here. I'm talking 'bout Bean Town shopping, baby."

"Well, how 'bout I leave you fifty G's and a first-class ticket back to Boston?" he asked. "That should hold you down 'til I get back."

Monica stood next to the bed with her hands on her hips, looking sexy as ever. "And when will that be, Mister?"

Lil Will, still having thoughts about laying her down and sexing her one more time before he left, replied, "When I'm done wrapping shit up down here."

"I can't keep doing this shit, Will," Monica said, eyes glossing over from the emotions she was feeling.

"Listen," he said after sighing, "you know what I do. You know what you were signing on to."

"Not this!" she snapped. "Nigga, I ain't trying to be a widow before I toss the flowers over my shoulder good."

Lil Will saw the point she was making. "I understand that. I'm telling you, it'll be over soon."

"When?" she countered. "You keep saying the same ole shit, Lil Will."

Lil Will's phone was vibrating on the lamp stand. "Hold on. This damn phone going crazy." He picked up the phone and answered. "Yeah."

"It's Mark," the caller said. "You need to get over here to Red's house now. Big problem, fam."

"I'm on the way," Lil Will said, looking Monica in the eyes. She was heated and he knew it. "Give me a minute, fam." He hung up the phone and tossed it on the bed. He hopped up out of the bed and pulled her close and tongued her down before saying, "Have a safe trip back. I love you, Monica."

Lil Will got dressed and hurried out the door. Whatever the problem was, he knew he wanted it to be over with already because he didn't want any bullshit fucking with his money.

****

Mark had hung up the phone and was back at it. "You know the rules, my nigga," he said to Mike-Mike, "and you broke rule number one."

"Come on, Mark," Mike-Mike said, scared half to death. "Them pigs had my ass in the swivel. Said if I didn't say shit, I was gettin 2 L's plus ten fo' the shit they got out of my house. Honestly, I didn't know I had so much work at my spot."

Mike-Mike had found himself in a sticky situation. He was one of Lil Will's runners who really liked to floss. The shit had caught up with him. The feds had kicked in his door and given him the ultimate ultimatum: either snitch, or his ass was going upstate.

Mark looked at him sideways. "So your ass been slipping?"

"No, fam," Mike-Mike answered nervously. "Listen, fam, I got a wife and kids with a hundred grand a year job. What was I supposed to do?"

"Keep yo' fuckin' mouth shut, Mike-Mike," Mark said harshly.

Mark hit him in the head with the pistol, sending blood splattering on the floor. Mike-Mike's face was already fucked up. Knots everywhere and his eyes were swollen shut. That last blow sent him unconscious.

One of Mark's men grabbed him by the neck. "Wake yo' bitch ass up. You gon' feel this shit, nigga."

Mike-Mike regained consciousness, but it was hard to focus on one thing. The pain kept him fading in and out. "Fuck! I'm sorry, bruh! I fucked up!"

Lil Will had walked in. He took one look at Mike-Mike and sighed, saying, "Mike-Mike, what's up? Nigga, I just missed a five star breakfast with a great piece of pussy on the platter, so start talking. What's the problem?"

"Fam," Mike-Mike said, shaking like a leaf on a tree, "I swear it wasn't me. The nigga Tony was dropping dimes."

"What?" Lil Will asked, interested in hearing more.

"Yeah," Mike-Mike said weakly. "Will, man, them folks had all the intel they needed on a nigga. They kicked in my door asking questions 'bout the whole crew."

"Okay," Lil Will said nonchalantly. "What did you tell 'em?"

Scared and nervous, Mike- Mike responded, saying, "Bruh, they told me I was goin' down on 2 L's plus ten fo' the weight a nigga holdin'."

"Nigga, that ain't what I asked you," Lil Will said in a cold tone. "What came out of yo' mouth?"

Mike-Mike flinched, knowing he was going to get hit with the pistol again. But when it didn't come, he spoke up. "I told 'em yo' name was Black and you was from D.C. Also that you was renting a room from me. I swear, fam, on everything, I ain't no rat."

Lil Will nodded silently, in deep thought. He asked Mark what he thought. Mark took one good look at Mike-Mike and said, "I think we should off the nigga. Talking is talking. No matter if ya giving up false intel or not. It might be a nigga that fits the dime ya dropped and Slaughter Boyz don't get down like that fo' a get out of jail free card. Nigga, this ain't Monopoly."

Lil Will was hearing the shit Mark was saying, but something wasn't right. He thought back to the night he and Mark were at the club, when he had to call a blackout because of the way Fred and Rimp acted. Then the thought hit him. How in the hell did they find their way to Boston and just so happen to be in the same spot? The nigga didn't believe in coincidence.

"Yo, check this out," Lil Will said to Mark. "Mark, when's the last time you seen Fred and Rimp?"

Mark thought for a minute before answering. "Fam, I ain't seen them since Friday at the club. Why?"

"Look. Find them niggas," Lil Will said angrily. "Put a hundred G's on them niggas' heads. Bring 'em in alive."

"A'ight, fam," Mark replied.

Lil Will looked at Mike-Mike. "Y'all clean this nigga up," he told Mark's jump out crew, "and put 80 G's in his pockets. Mike-Mike, you a good nigga. Sorry 'bout this misunderstanding."

As they untied Mike-Mike, he looked at Lil Will and said, "I understand. I'm just glad you a good judge of a nigga's loyalty to ya."

"Fo' sho'," Lil Will said. "But listen. Let me or Mark know if you need anything or if the alphabet boys come fuckin' with you again. Lay low fo' a minute."

"That's love, fam," Mike-Mike said.

"Fo' sho'," Lil Will said before turning his attention to Mark. "Mark, let me holla at ya."

They walked out of the room, leaving the others to clean Mike-Mike up.

Mark posted up on the wall out in the hallway and said, "What's on your mind, Lil Will?"

"I need you to take Mike-Mike and whoever else you choose and fly up to Boston," Lil Will said while putting the rest of the plan together in his mind. "Y'all can hold shit down up there while I handle this biz down here. Monica already headed back up. Make sho' she good."

"Gotcha, fam," Mark replied.

"'Preciate ya," Lil Will responded. "And Mark, let me do the thinking from here on."

****

The FBI had snatched Fred up. It looked like a real arrest to the public, which was what they wanted. Back at the station they took the cuffs off and offered Fred something to eat, drink, and smoke.

"Yeah," Fred said. "I'll have a steak and potato smothered in gravy. Make sho' my steak well done. I appreciate ya. Now what the fuck do you all want?"

His attitude was annoying to the agents, Scott and Dunlap.

"Shut the fuck up and listen, wannabe-ass nigga," Agent Dunlap demanded. "We want to know every move Lil Will makes and where he going to be before he knows it."

Fred was nervous. The thought of doing what they were asking scared him more than anything. "Man, y'all play some dirty-ass games. Y'all tryin' to get a nigga whacked? This nigga ain't slow. It's only a matter of time before he puts this shit in perspective."

"Sounds like your ass needs to get what we need then, Freddy," retorted Agent Scott.

Fred sighed, knowing he had stepped off into some deep shit. "I got you. Just give me a minute. I got to make sure I do it in a way where I can cover my own ass when this shit go down."

"You got thirty days," Agent Dunlap scolded. "Don't forget, we want him on the spot with the product. You got that?"

Shook up, Fred said, "Yeah, I understand."

"Let's leave this scary-ass nigga to his steak and potato, Agent Dunlap," said Agent Scott. "You know your way out."

"It's hard for me not to!" Fred yelled at the agents.

The agents walked out of the room just as his food arrived. Heated and in deep thought, Fred's conscience was fucking with him. Here he was being disloyal to a nigga who had been nothing but loyal to him and his family. And there was the other thought: his family.

The feds had him pinned him on some heavy shit that would have him down so long he'd be like a ghost of the past to the streets. Not to mention the baby he had on the way. He finished his meal and walked out, trying to figure out how to right his wrong, but he knew to tell Lil Will meant death.

Later on, still thinking about the best way to clear his conscience, Fred lay in bed tossing and turning. In no way was shit adding up for him, so he picked up the phone and hit Rimp.

"Fred, what's good, fam?" Rimp asked after answering the phone. "A nigga been trying to get at you all day. Where you at?"

Paranoid, Fred said, "I'm chilling in the room. Why? What's going on?"

"Something is going down. Everybody is to meet up tonight. Check yo' texts," Rimp said finally.

"Alright, my nigga. Bet," Fred responded.

They hung up. Fred, out of frustration, punched the wall. "Fuck! I can't go out like this. I got to let him know what's happening."

He hightailed out of the room so fast that he left his phone. He found himself at his baby mama Holly's crib. Without speaking, he ran into the bathroom and locked the door. She ran to the bathroom door.

"Fred, what's wrong?" Holly asked through the door.

"Too damn much!" he yelled back through the door. "You got to get away from here! I'm putting you on a plane to Miami! Stay with your moms for a while 'til I get this shit straight!"

Holly beat on the door. "Open this door and talk to me."

He unlocked the door. She saw the tears and worry in his eyes as he said, "I fucked up. I fucked up bad. You ain't safe 'round me, so you got to leave."

She embraced his head, holding him between her breasts, which were so soft.

"Okay, baby," was her response. "Everything is going to be okay. You'll straighten it out. I know you will."

"Holly, you don't understand how bad I've fucked up," Fred said. "Everything I did, I did for you and the baby."

"I know, Fred," she said in a soft tone of voice. "And we love you for everything you do."

He looked into her big brown eyes. Knowing it might be the last time he saw her, he took his time making love to her.

****

Bee had returned from D.C. Teddy was waiting on him to fill him in on everything.

"Bro," Teddy said, hyped up, "we 'bout to get this money. I already got a team guarding the warehouse."

"That's what's up," was Bee's response. "Where Dink at?"

Teddy hunched his shoulders in an "I don't give a fuck" way. "That nigga think just because he big bro he can show face when he get ready."

"Yeah," Bee said, "I know, fam. That's Dink for a nigga."

"Yeah. Well he better get some act right 'bout his self, 'cause shit 'bout to get real. And with the shit Will got riding on this, you know he ain't going fo' the fuck shit," Teddy said with certainty.

"Facts. Let's just make sho' shit stay straight," Bee said. "You heard me, Teddy?"

Teddy passed Bee the blunt and downed a shot of gin before he responded. "Yeah, bro. Just looking at this fuck nigga

Dre coming up in here like he run shit."

Bee waved the thought off. "Man, fuck that fool. Soon he'll be buying from us." Dre walked up on the scene and said, "Bee, what's up?"

"Shit," Bee said in a nonchalant way. "What's good, Dre?"

"Money," Dre said before turning his attention to Teddy. "What's up, Teddy?"

"What you said, my nigga," Teddy said quickly. "Money."

"That's not what I'm hearing," Dre said. "I hear the Slaughter Boyz on a takeover, and my block is on the list. I can't have that."

"Nigga, fuck what you hearing," Teddy said coldly.

As they stood, Dre's crew drew down on them. They stared down the barrels of 40s and AKs without showing any signs of fear.

"Look, nigga. Ain't nobody scared," Teddy said with a smile. "It ain't about pulling out on real niggas. Is you niggas capable of pulling the trigga?"

Dre laughed. "Oh believe me, they are. Sit down; let's talk."

"Nigga, it ain't shit to talk about," Teddy said with a look of hatred on his face.

Dre and his crew had slipped. While they were focused on Bee and Teddy, some S.M.F. niggas had crept up on them and drawn down. Dre felt the cold steel on the back of his head and said, "Damn. It's like that, my nigga?"

"Yeah, just like that," Teddy replied. "Now get the fuck out."

"Fo' sho', Teddy," Dre said while motioning for his crew to put their guns down. "We'll be seeing each other real soon."

"No pressure," said Teddy as the S.M.F. Boyz escorted Dre and his crew out. "Bee," Teddy started to say, "bro, I'm going to kill that nigga."

"I'm with it, replied Bee, "but let's talk about that shit tomorrow. I need to go handle something."

"Me too," Teddy said, looking at the time.

They went their separate ways. Teddy called Henry. "Henry, it's Teddy."

"What up? What's the move?" asked Henry.

He told him about the shit that just went down. "That's some crazy shit, my nigga," Henry said.

"Yeah," Teddy said. "That's why I need you to body this fool ASAP. You got it?"

"Yeah, I got it," answered Henry.

Teddy thought about the incident with him and Mike and asked, "By the way. Have you and Mike kissed and made up?"

"Hell no," Henry said angrily. "That nigga knows what it is."

"I feel you, my nigga," Teddy said, frustrated with the whole situation, "but you know that's my brother's mans an' them. I need you to dead that shit, fam. Fo' me."

"What about that nigga?" asked Henry. "What's his thinking like?"

"I'll get Bee to have a sit down with Mike," Teddy said, hoping shit would play out to everyone's advantage.

"Hmm... A'ight, fam. But if that nigga look at me sideways, I'm going to fuck his world up," Henry said confidently.

"Bet. One," Teddy replied.

They cut lines. Henry had to remember what he was headed to do. Looking at a bad redbone walking down the street triggered his memory. He called Sabrina. After three tries, she answered. "Hello?"

"Damn, bitch, where you at?" he asked.

"Henry, I'm at home," she replied. "Why?"

"I need to see you. I'll be there in a minute," he said.

"Nigga, how you know I ain't got company? A bitch is single," Sabrina shot back.

"They better be gone before I get there," Henry said in a demanding voice.

"Whatever," replied Sabrina before she hung up.

As he turned onto her street, he was thinking about her hard. She was fine and had business about herself, which was what he liked the most. Shit, every nigga appreciated that about a bitch.

He pulled up and hopped out of the Benz. Whoever had tailed him thought he wasn't on point, but just as soon as the two masked men got up on him, he pulled the Glock 40 and let loose, hitting one in the chest. The other one took off running and he ran after him, letting off rounds until the clip was empty.

Sabrina ran outside to see what was going on. The first thing she noticed was the body lying in her front yard, and she started screaming. By the time the porch light came on, Henry had made it back.

"Listen," he said, breathing hard from running, "go in the house and get yo' shit. You coming with me. Hurry up."

She did as she was told. As they turned off her street, the police were turning on. "What have you done?" she asked.

"Shit. I pulled up and the niggas jumped down on me." Henry's mind went somewhere else as he thought about what just happened. Hold up. Bitch, you tried to set me up?"

"What, nigga?" she said, surprised. "Really?"

"You was the only one I told I was coming over here," he snapped at her.

Sabrina sucked her teeth. "First of all, nigga, you just called me a hot-ass minute ago. How would I have time to get niggas to tail you? And a bitch don't get down like that."

Henry thought for a second, and she was right. "You dead ass right. My bad. So much shit going on, a nigga mind cloudy."

"Whatever," Sabrina said with a wave of her hand. "Where we goin'?"

"My spot. I got to call Teddy. It might be that fool Mike," Henry said.

He pulled out his phone and hit him on speed dial. Teddy

answered, "What's up, my nigga?"

"I just bodied a nigga," was Henry's response

"Come again," replied Teddy, making sure he heard right.

"You heard me," Henry shot back. "I just bodied a nigga."

"Where? What happened?" Teddy asked with panic in his voice.

"I pulled up at Sabrina's house and two niggas who were masked up tried to get at me," Henry replied.

"What the fuck?" Teddy snapped out of frustration. "You good?"

"Yeah. I'm headed to my spot now," Henry said.

"Okay. Okay. Lay low, my nigga. I'm going to see what's going on and let you know. One," Teddy said before hanging up the phone.

Teddy's mind went back to the confrontation he had just gotten into with Dre and his crew. He knew where they kicked it. He jumped in his ride and swerved over to the Eastside. He pulled up on the side of the corner store and parked out of sight.

Teddy opened the glove compartment and pulled out the two automatic 9 mm. He checked to make sure both clips were full before getting out of the car and creeping up on the scene. Dre had his back turned, serving a fiend, and most of his crew were too damn drunk to pay attention to what was about to go down. On the side of the building, Teddy checked his guns over one last time before he rounded the corner and let loose.

"This is what real niggas do! Fuck niggas, it's on sight!"

Teddy made sure he popped Dre. He emptied half of the clip in him as he tried to run. He caught a few of his homeboys. By the time both clips were empty, the set was a ghost town besides the dead bodies.

Teddy ran back to his car, jumped in, and fled the scene before the police arrived.

Willie Slaughter

Chapter Seven

Mark had decided it was best for him to stay with Lil Will, so he sent word for his right hand man to hold shit down in Boston.

"Damn, fam! I didn't know Albany was piped up like this," Mark said, excited.

"Bruh, you ain't really seen shit yet," Lil Will replied, laughing.

They loaded up the car.

"The whole southwest to Florida going to be in our pockets," Lil Will said to Mark before yelling at his brother. "Yo, Teddy!"

Teddy came trotting over to the car. "What's good, big bro?"

"Us," Lil Will replied. "Get everybody together, and meet us at the spot ASAP."

"You back?" Teddy asked enthusiastically.

"Yup, and it's time," was Lil Will's response.

"That's what I'm talking about," Teddy said happily and he jumped on the phone.

Lil Will and Mark finished loading up and before they got in, Lil Will told Mark to tell the driver to stop by his mom's house.

"Got you," was Mark's reply.

They pulled up in front of his mother's crib. She was sitting on the front porch until he got out. Smiling, with tears in her eyes, she walked off the porch to meet him. "My baby home! Thank you God! Baby, look at you. Who these people? The feds or something?"

"No ma'am. These are my people." Lil Will introduced them. "Mama, this is Mark. And Mark, this is my mama, Ms. Ruby."

Lil Will's mother, Ms. Ruby, was a fairly short brown-skinned woman who seemed to embody a great amount of strength. Although a woman of faith, she never looked down on her sons about anything they did in the streets.

"Nice to meet you, Ms. Ruby," Mark said, shaking her hand.

"Nice to meet you too. Come on in. I just cooked some greens and fried chicken," she replied.

"That's what I'm talking about," Lil Will said and he walked in the house, followed by Mark and his mother.

They sat at the dining table and enjoyed their meal. "Mama, where my sister at?" Lil Will asked his mother.

She waved her hand in the air. "Please, baby, don't talk them up. In my car somewhere. They running ya mama crazy is what they doing."

"You still going to the Mud Puddle?" he asked.

"Every chance I get. We don't stop having fun just because you all think we are getting too old," she replied.

"Now you know you getting too old for that," he said jokingly.

"Boy, ain't nothing old about me. I still got it," she said while doing a little grooving.

They laughed. Mark, knocking off his plate, complimented her cooking, saying, "Ms. Rudy, you definitely can throw down in the kitchen."

"Thank you," she replied, "but I want you to know it ain't free. That plate gon' cost you a hundred dollars."

"How 'bout I give you two?" Mark asked, reaching in his front pocket.

"Okay," Ms. Ruby said. She held her hand out to Lil Will. "That goes for you too, son. Pay up."

"You ain't changed a bit, Mama," Lil Will said.

They laughed, ate, and talked for a while. Mark excused himself to give Lil Will some alone time with his mother.

"Here you go, Mama," Lil Will said as he handed her a black bag.

She looked at her son. "What's this, baby?"

"Eighty thousand," he said.

Her eyes got big. "Damn. Y'all don't want another plate? What about the guys in the car? For this, you can take it all with you."

"Nah, Mama," he said, laughing. "We good. Just wanted to put something in your pockets."

She opened the bag and peeped inside of it. "Well, you did that."

They hugged. Lil Will checked the time. "Well, let me go. I got to meet Teddy and everybody else."

"Tell my boys hello for me," she said.

"I will. Have a blessed day, Mama," he added.

"You too. I love you," Ms. Ruby said.

"Love you too, Mama," Lil Will said before getting into the car.

****

Teddy, Bee, Dink, and the crew were at the warehouse waiting on Lil Will. Bee was a little wary of the fact Lil Will had left it on Dink to handle certain business matters.

"Bruh, is everything in play?" Bee asked Dink.

"Yeah," answered Dink. "I got the North. Teddy get Southwest. Bee, you got East up."

Bee nodded his head, feeling his territory. "Good. I can visit Savannah, GA. I got people there already lined up with that check."

"It's good to see everybody here," Lil Will walked in and said.

Lil Will had shown up. He pounded his brothers up. He looked at the boxes which the product was in. "I had three tons of work shipped here. Do the math. That's forty million, three thousand bricks going at twenty five a pop, plus pills. We starting N.W.A. here all the way to Boston. It's time to take out everyone that thinks they own the streets.

"The street belongs to us. Slaughter Boyz. This our shit.

Every corner."

"Shit sounds good, bruh," Teddy cut in. "But what about the police?"

"What about them?" Lil Will shot back? "They work fo' us. I got them. Y'all just focus on getting this shit sold."

"Are we fucking with the heroin too?" asked Dink.

"Fuck no," snapped Lil Will. "That boy brings the feds. Nigga trying to eat. Not get ate, Dink. We got everything we need to get on top and stay on top. Clean cut coke. We utilize every ally we got. The Wolf Pack, S.M.F. We got it all. The future belongs to us."

"Nigga," Dink stressed, "let's get this shit over with. I got shit to do. Money to be made."

"Dink, chill, big bro," Bee said.

The shit was irking Dink. He was used to giving orders, not taking them.

"Bee, you got your people on line and ready?" Lil Will asked his brother.

"Yeah," he answered quickly, "my zone on point. All I'm waiting for is the work."

Lil Will turned towards his other brother Teddy and looked him in the eyes. "What about you, Teddy?"

"You know I got mines. Matter of fact, I've been thinking about expanding my territory farther south," Teddy said eagerly.

Lil Will looked at his oldest brother out of the corner of his right eye. "And Dink?"

"Nigga, don't ask me no dumb-ass shit like that. I been holding shit down," Dink replied.

Everybody looked at Dink. Lil Will stood and walked up on him. "Listen, bruh. This my show. You in or out? It's your call. At the end of the day, you still my big brother, but don't ever disrespect me again. We good?"

Lil Will's killers clutched with eyes up on Dink and his crew, ready to body them.

"Nigga, fuck you," Dink said coldly. "You need me, I don't need you. I run my shit. Believe that, bruh."

Lil Will pointed towards the door. "Like I said. The door is open."

"Yeah, I see," Dink replied sarcastically. "We'll holla."

Dink and his crew dipped.

A little heated, Lil Will asked, "Anybody else want to leave?" Nobody moved. "Good," was his response to their silence. "Let's get this money. Teddy, you and Bee, let me holla at you."

They strolled over to a corner away from everyone else.

"Do y'all think y'all can push Dink's load?" Lil Will asked his brothers.

"No problem, bruh," said Bee.

"Man," Teddy started saying, "we all know how Dink is. Nigga power struck. He'll come 'round."

"You ain't never lied," Lil Will said, laughing.

They all knew their oldest brother. He'd been the same since they were young. He had the mind for running the show, but his ego always got in the way of his better judgement.

"Whether he comes around or not," Lil Will said, "we are going to stack this paperwork from the ground up."

****

Rimp had been trying to catch up with Fred, and when he finally did, they sat in the club blowing dro and drinking in VIP.

"What you been up to, Fred?" asked Rimp. "You a hard nigga to catch up with these days."

Paranoid, Fred said, "A lot on my mind. Nigga, we got a major problem. I got word that Mark and Lil Will got a ticket on a nigga's head."

"Yeah. A hundred thousand," Rimp added.

"Damn. Where you get that info?" Fred said, surprised.

"Last night with Rick. We gave him all the money," said Rimp. "I wonder what the shit is about."

"For real, my nigga," Fred stated.

Fred's heart was pounding in his chest and he started to sweat. "We got to see what's up and why they at a nigga."

"Yeah. Fo' sho', fam," agreed Rimp.

"Listen," Fred said nervously, "my baby mama going through some shit. I got to check on her. You make some calls to see what you can find out on your end. We'll get up later on."

"A'ight, my nigga," said Rimp.

Fred left out in a hurry.

Damn, that nigga acting strange, Rimp thought to himself as he downed the shot of Remy. He exited the club, hopped in his Lexus, and drove off.

Driving down 15th Street, he started making calls. He wasn't paying attention to the black van coasting behind him. As he stopped at the four-way red light, three masked men jumped out of the van with guns pointing at him.

"Get out the car, nigga!" yelled the masked gunman with the gun pointed at Rimp's head. "Don't make me ask yo' bitch ass twice!"

He got out and two of them escorted him back to the van. Before he could ask what was going on, his whole world went black. The third man hopped in the Lexus and followed them.

"Wake up, nigga!" one of the gunmen yelled as he kicked Rimp in the side. "Wake yo' ass up!"

Rimp came back to. He tried to move, but they had him hogtied. He was madder at himself for slipping when he knew a price tag was on his head. "A'ight, nigga. I'm awake," said Rimp.

"Where Fred at?" asked the gunman.

"Nigga, fuck you!" screamed Rimp.

The masked gunman kicked him in the ribs so hard he

could hardly breathe. "One last time. Where Fred at?"

"Fuck you, my nigga," Rimp said painfully.

The gunman pistol whipped him, causing blood to fly everywhere in the back of the van. "Is it still fuck me, nigga? Where he at?"

Rimp blacked out again from the pain. His head and face were gashed up and bloody.

"Man, fuck this nigga!" The gunman put the pistol to his head and was about to squeeze the trigger until the other man stopped him.

"Nah, fool!" he yelled. They want this nigga alive. Not dead."

"Damn." The angry gunman put away the nine millimeter. "My bad."

****

Monica was happy; however, she was sad to be home. Her mind was on her man. Knowing she had to break out of it, she decided to go shopping. While she was debating with herself about who to take with her, the phone rang. It was Erica.

"Hey girl. I heard you was back in town," Erica said.

Erica was Monica's home girl from the sandbox days all the way through college. She was five foot even, chocolate, and thick in all of the right places.

"Erica, I was just about to call you," said Monica.

"Girl, please," Erica said sarcastically. "I haven't heard from you in six months."

Doing the math in her head, Monica said, "Damn, it's been that long?"

"Yep," she replied.

"Anyways," Monica started to say, "you want to go to the mall?"

Erica laughed. "Girl, my money funny. You keep forgetting

I got four girls."

"You good, Erica. It's on me. I got you," Monica said.

"Fo' real?" her homegirl said with enthusiasm. "I'll meet you there at 2. I got to find somebody to keep these bad-ass kids."

"Okay," Monica said, laughing. "I'll see you soon."

Monica hung up. As she went upstairs to get ready for a shower, she scanned through her unread text messages and saw she had one from K.C. "Damn," she said to herself with a smile. It had been twelve years since she'd heard from him.

She opened the text that read, "Hey Monica, it's K.C., the light-skinned green-eyed nigga that told you no matter what I will always find your sexy ass. Can we have dinner tonight?'

Now how did he manage to find me after all this time? she thought to herself. She showered with him on her mind. Dinner with him won't be all that bad, she thought. She dried off and got fresh for her girls' day out.

She pulled up in the mall's parking lot. As she parked, her phone vibrated. She answered, "Hello?"

"I see your car," Erica said.

"Good," replied Monica.

She hopped out and walked over to the entrance door where Erica was standing. Seeing Monica, she said, "Bitch, it's hot as hell out here."

They laughed and hugged.

"Bitch, come on!" Monica yelled. "Let's shop!"

They went through the mall on a shopping spree.

Tee and his partner Ju-Ju watched them from a distance.

"Damn, Tee, this shit gon' be double the pleasure," Ju-Ju said, licking his lips.

"You ain't lying, my nigga," Tee said, keeping his eyes on them. "Two bad-ass bitches."

"Fo' sho'," Ju-Ju replied. "But let's not forget the mission, my nigga. We out to get paid. That bitch Monica is Lil Will's girl."

"Sweet," Tee commented. "Let's pull up, my nigga."

Monica and Erica made their way around the mall at least twice before they called it a day. "Damn, a bitch feet tired from fuckin' with you, Monica," Erica said playfully. "What time is it?"

Monica looked at her pink diamond Citizen watch and said, "Bitch, we only shopped for five hours."

"A'ight, bitch," Erica said. "You going to pay my babysitter?"

"Shit, I forgot," Monica said honestly. "My bad, homegirl. Let's go."

Ten thousand dollars later, they walked out carrying their bags.

"Hold up, ladies," Ju-Ju said as he and his partner walked up. "Let us help y'all with that."

They paused in stride as the two men approached. Erica didn't have a problem with relieving her hands, arms, and shoulders of her bags. Not wanting to be stank about it, Monica let the other guy carry hers.

"I'm Ju-Ju and this my nigga, homie Tee," Ju-Ju said, introducing him and his partner.

"I'm Monica and that's Erica," Monica said politely. "I appreciate your assistance, but I ain't single. I got a man."

That still didn't stop Ju-Ju from being a gentleman about the situation. He and Tee carried the bags and made small talk with Monica and Erica along the way. They made it to her car and put the bags in. Ju-Ju looked around and asked Monica, "Where he at?"

She frowned and said, "Excuse me?"

"You said you got a man," he said. "Where is he?"

"Out of town, handling business, if you must know," she responded with a mild touch of sarcasm.

"No way in hell I'd be anywhere without you by my side if you was mines," Ju-Ju rebounded smoothly.

"Thanks for the compliment," Monica replied.

"Your sexy ass deserves it and more. Give me a chance to show you how much more you deserve," he pleaded.

She looked at Erica, who was enjoying the attention she was getting from the other man. "Listen," she said to Ju-Ju, "as you can see, we're having a girls' day out. Niggas not included. Besides, I got to get my homegirl back home to her kids."

Ju-Ju opened the door for her. "Just keep a nigga in mind."

"Probably not," said Monica before screaming at her homegirl. "Erica, bring yo' ass on!"

She jumped in on the passenger side and they drove off. Erica was hyped up from her conversation with Tee and said, "Damn, girl. You see them fine-ass niggas?"

"Kind of hard not to. They slid up with that weak-ass pickup game," said Monica.

They laughed. She dropped Erica off and made her way home. As she lay in the bed, she thought about what Ju-Ju had said and tried calling Lil Will. All she got was voicemail.

"Damn, bae. I haven't heard from you in a week. What's up?"

She hung up and thought to herself, *My mama told me about niggas like this. Don't be so quick to give up the goodies. Make them wait and work for it. Damn, I played myself.* She cried herself to sleep.

The next morning she got ready for work with her mind made up. If the nigga didn't live up to her vision of him, she was gone. *God knows what he's doing and two can play that game*, she thought to herself.

****

As Erica dropped her kids off at school, her phone rang. She answered. "Hello?"

"Hey sexy eyes. How are you?" a male voice said.

"Who is this?" Erica asked.

"The nigga you know you need to be with," the man replied.

"I know a lot of niggas who want to wife a bitch," she snapped.

"Well damn. I need to get my shit together. How about I take you to breakfast?" the man proposed.

"Maybe. Maybe not. Depends on who I'm talking to," she said girlishly.

"It's Tee," he said. "You didn't save my number in yo' phone?"

"Only numbers in my phone are my homegirls, job, baby daddy, and babysitter. Everybody else is suspect," Erica shot back.

"Damn, Erica, I like yo' flava. So, what's up? We doing breakfast so we can talk face to face? A nigga ain't seen yo' sexy ass since the mall and we been texting all night the past few days," said Tee.

"A'ight, boo. You picked the right day because I'm off from work," said Erica

"Great," he responded happily. "Meet me at Ann's Café on 18th Street in ten minutes."

"I'm on my way, boo," she replied sexually. "Bye." She hung up.

Tee went through his contacts, found Ju-Ju's number, and called him.

"Yo," Ju-Ju said, answering his phone.

"I'm about to have breakfast with Erica," Tee told him.

"Good," said Ju-Ju. "See what you can find out about Lil Will. I'm waiting on his bitch to get at me. She's the key we need to make this shit go smooth."

"I really don't think the nigga got a stash there," Tee said. "The nigga ain't slow by a long shot. I'll tell Erica to set some shit up. See if she can talk her friend into hooking up on a double date."

67

"That's the move. Just be smart, and play it cool, my nigga," Ju-Ju said, sounding concerned.

"No pressure," Tee said as he looked up and saw her coming. "Here come Erica. I'll holla at ya."

Tee hung up and hopped out of his ride. His eyes were glued on her the whole time. Her five foot even, one hundred forty pound frame, long black hair, and fat jiggling ass was perfection.

And to think she has kids, he thought to himself as he walked up and said, "What's good, sexy? I'm glad you could make it." He grabbed her hand and kissed it. "Let's eat. I'm starving. More so for a taste of you."

They walked in holding hands and making small talk which continued as they ate. "Erica, can we do this more often?" asked Tee. "And what's the deal with yo' homegirl?" he asked. "Is she like you?"

"And what is that supposed to mean?" she said with attitude.

"My nigga is a good dude and he feeling shorty," was his reply.

"Dead issue," was Erica's blunt response. "She's in love with her man Lil Will."

"Understood," said Tee. "My boy just trying to take her out and show her a good time. You know, have a li'l fun since her man ain't in town. We all can hook up and kick it. You think you can talk her into it?"

"Say that I can," Erica said seductively. "What you going to do for me?"

"Oh. It's like that?" he shot back.

"Something like that," she said.

They laughed. He leaned across the table and kissed her soft lips. For a second, she seemed all in, but then she pushed him back. "Slow your roll, boy. I got to go."

They locked eyes for what seemed like forever. It took a lot of willpower for her to break the stare. Out the door and back in her car, she was able to breathe easy again.

She looked at her phone and saw Monica had tried to hit her up. She called her back. "My bad, Monica."

"Bitch, where you been?" asked Monica. "I been texting and calling yo' ass for a minute."

Erica scrolled through her missed calls list. "I see. I had left my phone in the car."

"So how did it go?" Monica pried.

"He straight. We talked," was her modest answer.

"Bitch, quit tryin' to sound all grown up about it. Give me the tea," demanded Monica.

"Girl, the nigga might be my soulmate," Erica said all girly. "We got so much in common. We cool."

"What do he do? Where the nigga from?" asked Monica.

"Jersey," she replied.

"Let me guess," Monica said while thinking, "he's here on business? What about Ju-Ju? What's up with him? He don't sound like a Jersey nigga."

Erica laughed. "It's funny that you asked about him because he definitely wants to get to know you. And he knows about Will, but bitch, you need to get out and have some fun. Hell, he might be doing the same thing in GA."

Erica gave her something to think about. She knew nine times out of ten she was right. It was time for her to do her.

"Okay. Let's go out tonight," said Monica.

"Bitch, stop playin'!" Erica yelled.

"I'm dead ass. I need to get out and get my mind right," Monica said.

"Okay. I know the spot. Just be at my house at ten," Erica responded quickly.

"Bet that up. I'll see you then, homegirl," Monica said before she hung up, smiling as she thought it was all about her tonight.

Willie Slaughter

Chapter Eight

Mark and Lil Will cruised the streets of Albany. Due to the fact it was summertime, all the bad bitches were sporting two-piece bikini suits and shit of that nature. Mark was having a field day.

"Fam, this shit is different from up top," Mark said.

"Yeah, I know," was Lil Will's response.

"These bitches thick as fuck," Mark said while watching a group of broads stroll down the street, asses hanging out of the bottoms of the cutoff jean shorts and jiggling like Jell-O.

"True," Lil Will said, cutting his eyes at Mark, "but don't let 'em fool you. They'll be deep in yo' pockets while fuckin' and suckin' you to yo' satisfaction."

They had pulled up at the club. Inside, it was packed with bad bitches.

"This is the Fox," said Lil Will. "My nigga run it, so we 'bout to get lifted."

The hoes were watching them closely. Some of them watched to see who they were going to fuck and get money out of, and others just dancing, having a ball.

"In here, you better know how to hit," Lil Will yelled to Mark over the music. "It goes down. You got niggas from C.M.E., Chop Shop Boyz, D.D.B., Eastside, and Front Street. My nigga, we with The Southside. We the deepest."

While niggas were making their presence known, they were on the hoes. Lil Will was walking through, gone on the gas and drink, when he bumped into a dark-skinned broad. They looked at each other.

"Damn! Watch where you goin', girl!" he yelled.

"Nah, nigga! Watch where you goin'!" she yelled back.

Before he could respond, Mark came up and tapped him on the shoulder and said, "Ain't that ya brotha Dink over there?"

He looked and said, "Yeah!"

"Looks like shit about to get real for him," said Mark.

He turned back to the dark-skinned sister in front of him and said, "I'm going to catch up with you later!"

He strolled onto the dance floor to see what the move was. The nigga his brother was having words with looked like a bouncer or like he belonged in the NFL. Either way, he grabbed two double deuce bottles and eased up behind his brother to hear what was being said.

"Li'l nigga, you called my girl a bitch," the big dude said as he squared off with Dink.

"And?" Dink said, drunk as hell.

"And, nigga, I'll fuck you up," the big nigga said as he rushed toward Dink.

And without hesitation, Lil Will caught him by surprise. He broke both bottles over his head. Next thing you know, the S.M.F. niggas were all over his ass and the Front Street Boys were on the C.M.E. niggas as well.

The lights came on. Niggas were getting stomped out. Some were stabbed and the rest were running out of the building. It looked like a real crime scene. Blood was everywhere in puddles on the floor.

Lil Will grabbed his brother's drunk ass and Mark. They fled the scene as the semi-automatics started sounding off. Once they were a good distance away, he called Dink. "Bruh, you good?"

"Yeah, these niggas always want some smoke 'bout a bitch," Dink said, voice slurred.

"Shit happens," said Lil Will. "Take yo' drunk ass home, big bruh. We'll get up tomorrow."

"A'ight, Will. One, fam," Dink replied. He hung up.

Mark started laughing and said, "Nigga, you called that shit out."

"Yeah. A nigga done worked up an appetite," Lil Will said. "Swing by Krystal's."

They got to Crystals and it was packed. Mark looked at the long line at the drive thru and those who were inside, and said,

"Damn. We gon' be here all night tryin' to eat."

Lil Will laughed. "Nigga, this is where everybody comes after the club. I'm 'bout to catch one of these broads."

"Speaking of females," Mark started to say, "have you talked to Monica?"

It dawned on him. "Hell no. Fuck, fam, I've been so focused on this move a bitch ain't crossed my mind. I know she mad as hell. Let me call her crazy ass."

"Yeah, you do that while I go inside and get the grub," Mark said and hopped out.

Lil Will hit her up. The phone rang and rang. After the fourth try he gave up and decided he'd try again tomorrow.

As he looked up, he saw his partner Richard Boy pull up. He jumped out and strolled over to greet him.

"What up, my nigga," Lil Will said.

"Damn," Richard Boy said, seeing Lil Will. "What up, homie? You don't call to let a nigga know you in town?"

"Got a lot going on," said Lil Will.

"Shit," Richard Boy commented, "I was with yo' brotha the first time you came down."

"Word," said Lil Will.

"Yeah," he stated, "and nigga, I want in."

"Richard, you know I got you," Lil Will said as he pulled a wad of cash out of his pocket. "Here."

He gave him a thousand and told him to get at him tomorrow. As he turned to walk back to his ride, he caught sight of the dark-skinned female he'd bumped into at the club. She and a friend hopped out of a platinum 2013 Benz. *Dammit, man*, he thought to himself. There was something about her he couldn't quite put a finger on, but he felt like one day she would be his. As he was in deep thought, Mark hopped in with the food. He'd seen the same females, but didn't say shit.

"Man, that's that," said Mark.

"Yeah," Lil Will said, still caught up in his thoughts, "that's the one right there."

"Well, I got this broad I'm 'bout to meet at the room," Mark said.

"Okay," Lil Will replied. "You don't waste time, fam."

Mark chuckled. "Fo' what? I'm 'bout to dig deep off up in this GA pussy. Is Monica good?"

"She didn't answer," he replied.

"Damn, fam, it's all good. It's late. You know she works a 9 to 5 fo' hers," Mark said, trying to ease the tension.

"Yeah. Just drop me off at my mama's house. We'll get up in the morning," Lil Will said in deep thought.

"Fo' sho', fam," Mark said.

They sat in the parking lot of Crystal's, enjoying the burgers and fries and the view of every grade-A broad who found their way into their line of sight.

****

"Aye, pussy nigga, I need to holla at cha," Teddy yelled at Tony.

Teddy had laid on Tony. He finally caught him at home. As he came out of his crib, Teddy was shoving him back through the front door.

"Nigga, where my money?" he asked.

"Chill, homie," Tony said, scared as hell. "I got ya money. Some of it. But I'll have the rest soon."

"What the fuck you mean?" asked Teddy.

"I took a hit," Tony replied.

"And what in the hell that got to do with me?" Teddy asked. "Look, Tony, you got until Friday to have my shit or it's gon' be an early 4th of July 'round this bitch. Understand?"

"I got ya, bruh," Tony said, shaking.

"Word from the wise: have all of my money," Teddy said calmly.

Teddy's phone vibrated on his hip. He had a text saying they had a meeting at 2:30. *Damn*, he thought to himself. But so what? Everybody was making good money and they were back on top.

He showed up at the spot not a minute too late. Everybody was kicking the shit, blazing Cali bud and sipping on good.

"Now that everybody's here," Lil Will started to say, "let's get down to business. I called y'all here to let ya know proud I am of this family. I see everybody doing their thing, eating in these streets. We got to keep networking and building and remember, don't bring heat to the family unless it's necessary. Reports?"

Bee rose to his feet. "Word is them Florida niggas on some real live bullshit and they tryin' to find out who S.M.F. is."

"Easily handled," said Lil Will. "Anybody else?"

Teddy and Dink stood, but Teddy gave his report first. "Word is the drug unit looking at four of our spots. Supposed to go down soon."

"A'ight," Lil Will said, still thinking. "Tell whoever runnin' shit to lay low and keep shit clean as a whistle."

"Bet," Teddy replied before sitting back down.

"Dink, what up, big bruh?" asked Lil Will.

"Me and my bitch that works at the courthouse was at the Days Inn. She told me the county putting together a gang task force," was Dink's report.

Lil Will let everything he'd just learned soak in before speaking. "Okay... The only thing I see a problem with is how the fuck the drug unit knows about our spots. Somebody's talking. Find out, Dink."

"On it, bruh," Dink said.

"The rest of the shit is just a li'l gun play," Lil Will reminded them, "and we'll pay a few pigs to keep us informed on shit. Other than that, I got to hit the road. Lay low until I get back. The next shipment will be here before I return, so you three need to be on point. You'll be hearing from me the beginning of next week."

****

"Brina, what's up, girl?" asked Sopia.

"Shit, tryin' to find a bitch to do my hair," answered Sabrina. "What's up with you, Sopia?"

"Bitch, it's going down at the track on 300. Everybody going to be out there. Even them Slaughter Boyz," Sopia said, all hyped up.

"Bitch, why you so late with the info?" snapped Sabrina.

"Better late than never," she shot back sarcastically. "You know I'm going just to see Lil Will's fine ass on that fly-ass bike he got."

Thinking about all of the ballers who would be there, Sabrina said, "Damn. I'm about to go get my nails done now. Have you talked to Kerria?"

"Nah, not today," Sopia said. "Why?"

"I was just worried about her," Sabrina said in a serious tone. "She ain't been herself lately."

Sopia thought for a second. "Yeah, I noticed that too. We might need to pull up on our home girl."

"Fine with me," Sabrina said

Sopia looked at the time. "My break almost over with. Let me try to call my baby before he leaves out. We'll talk when I get off."

"A'ight, homegirl," Sabrina said.

Sopia hung up and voice command dialed Lil Will's number. His phone went straight to voicemail.

"You have reached The King. Leave a message. Beep."

"Hey boo. I'm just calling to see if we can get up before you leave GA. Muah!"

She hung up. It was obvious to her how much she loved

him. In her eyes, nothing would ever come between them. Nothing or nobody.

****

"Man, I'm on my way now," Henry said and hung up. He drove up the dirt road and stopped in front of the car parked sideways on the road. He checked his gun before he jumped out.

"What's up, Nod?" asked Henry.

"Let's talk," Nod said in a strictly business tone of voice.

Nod was a D.C. nigga who was heartless when it came to getting paid. If the price was right. consider the job done no matter who had to die. He had done a job for Henry in the past. His skills had proved to come in handy.

"Do you have what I asked for?" he asked Henry. "I need a picture and 50 G's up front and the rest when the job is done."

"Done," Henry assured him. "Just make sho' this shit don't fall back on me."

"Don't worry," Nod said with confidence. "My shit legit and I'm good at what I do."

"Good," Henry said, satisfied. "Everything you need is in the bag."

Nod picked the bag up and left. Henry got back in his ride and busted a U. *Mike, you a dead nigga*, he thought to himself. Feeling the need to enjoy himself, he called Sabrina.

"Hello," answered Sabrina.

"Hey sexy," he replied.

"Hey boo. What's up?" she asked.

"Feeling like money and fun," he said, feeling himself.

"I'm with it," Sabrina said softly. "You on your way home?"

"Yeah just 'bout to stop by the store. You need anything?"

he asked.

"Bring me whatever you think I want, bae," was her response.

"In that case," he said seriously, "I'll buy the fucking store."

She laughed. Her voice and mannerisms were so grown and sexy to him.

"Bye Henry. I'll see you when you get here," she said before hanging up the phone.

The line went dead. He went in the store and bought some blunts and some wine coolers. As he was about to leave, he saw Mike pulling up. He wanted so badly to body the nigga himself, but didn't want to get his hands dirty with all the money being made. He watched as Mike and three more men walked across the parking lot, talking.

"Man, we almost had that nigga the other night," the guy on the left side of Mike said.

"Yeah, so you say," Mike said angrily. "If you would've waited two more seconds, he would be dead. Nigga, next time do the job right."

After hearing that, Henry was amped up. He grabbed his pistol and opened the door, about to let loose, when his phone rang. He looked at the caller ID. It was his mama. *Nigga, next time we meet, you dead*, he thought as he closed the door and answered the phone. "Hey Mama."

"Baby, I'm sorry for calling you so late," his mother swore.

"It's okay, Mama. What's wrong? Are you okay?" he asked, concerned.

"I'm good. It's your father. We at the hospital now," she said.

"Is he okay?" Henry asked.

"I don't know. Nobody told me nothing yet. And he been in the back for over four hours now," she said, worried.

"I'm on my way, Mama," he said.

He hung up. His mother and father had been tight for 37

years. Even though he had four children outside of their marriage, two of whom he didn't even know, his mother loved him because no matter what he did in the streets, his father always took care of home first.

Henry didn't waste time looking for a parking spot. He pulled up next to the Emergency Room entrance and hopped out and ran inside, where he greeted and hugged his mother. Her eyes were puffy from crying.

"Sit down, Mama. Where everybody at?" he asked.

"They're on the way," she said as she looked up towards the emergency room entrance door. "Here they come now."

His two sisters and younger brother came in the door in a hurry. They all hugged their mother. After they tried to cheer each other up, the doctor walked up and stood before them. By his facial expression, Henry already knew.

"Mrs. Knight," he said.

She rose to her feet. "Yes, I'm Mrs. Knight. Is my husband okay?"

The doctor shook his head and said, "I'm sorry, Mrs. Knight. We did what we could. With his health condition and age, the heart attack was too much on him. I'm sorry to say that he didn't make it."

"Oh my Lord! My God!" she screamed.

His mother's knees gave and she fell to the floor in tears, yelling. Henry was motionless. The doctor called a nurse to check on his mother. After making sure she was okay, he left them at the hospital. He hated the world at the moment.

He pulled up at his spot around two thirty in the morning, drained. He hadn't expected Sabrina to still be up, but she was. One look into her eyes and his tears poured like a waterfall.

"What's wrong, Henry? Talk to me," she demanded.

He was too choked up on his tears to respond.

"You scaring me, Henry. What's going on? What happened?" she asked, afraid.

"He...he...he's gone," was all he could muster up the

strength to say.

"Who? Who you talking about?" she asked.

"My pops," he finally managed to get out between sobs.

She pulled him close to her and rocked him like was a baby. "I'm so sorry, baby. What happened?"

"I just left the hospital. They say it was a heart attack," he explained

. "I'm so sorry, Henry," Sabrina said sincerely.

"It's okay. I mean, I love my pops," Henry stated.

"Listen, Henry," she said, "you got to be strong. Yo' family need you to be strong. I need you to be strong."

"I know. I'm sorry, Sabrina. I ain't usually no emotional-ass nigga. The shit just hurts when it hits home," he said.

"It's cool. A bitch don't want a nigga to be hard 24/7. I'm here for you. Come on. Let's go upstairs," Sabrina said. She grabbed him by the hand and led him upstairs to the bathroom. "Sit right here while I run you some bath water. It will help, okay?"

"A'ight," Henry said as he sat down on the side of the bed.

Hearing the running water made his mind wander. He thought about his family and the effects his father death was going to have on them all. Then his mind went to Mike and the conversation he had overheard. The shit just fueled his anger. All he could picture was how many way he could kill him and get away with it clean.

****

Lil Will and Mark were on their way back to Boston. He'd asked Mark about some unfinished business. Immediately, he jumped on the phone, talked for a minute, and hung up.

"They know we're on our way," Mark said. "They say Rimp ain't talking."

Lil Will acted like he didn't even hear what he said about Rimp. "What's the word on Fred?"

"Nobody seen him," replied Mark.

"Mark, we need both of 'em to get to the bottom of this shit," Lil Will said, sounding a little frustrated.

"I'm on it," Mark said.

Lil Will knew Rimp. The nigga was more gangsta than the majority of the niggas he knew. He would die before he showed any sign of disloyalty.

"Fam, send some niggas to get at this nigga's mama, sister, grandma. I don't give a fuck. Just flush this nigga out so we can get this shit behind us," Lil Will said.

"Say no more. Consider it done," Mark said as he jumped back on the phone.

Mark called a few people and gave them the go ahead. "Done. Don't you think you should call Monica?"

He didn't answer, but he did call her.

This time, she answered. "Hey."

"Everything good?" Lil Will asked, "I been calling you. Where you been?"

"I been around. I called you too, but I see you didn't have time for me nor did you try to make time. So I went out a couple nights with Erica," she said.

"Really?" Lil Will said, sounding surprised.

"Yeah," Monica said. "Look, Will, I love you with all my heart, but I'm not going to keep being your fool."

"Monica, a lot been - "

"Save it," Monica cut him off mid-sentence. "I ain't trying to hear that same old tired-ass story."

"Damn. It's like that?" he snapped.

"Yep," Monica said.

"Listen," Lil Will said roughly, "I don't know what bitch or nigga filled yo' head up with this amped up shit, but you better watch you tone or - "

"Or what, Will?" she yelled through the phone. "You going to do what? Just like I thought."

"You just hold that thought 'til a nigga get there," he said, heated.

"Don't bring yo' ass to my house!" she yelled.

"Your house? Bitch, you mean my house. I paid for that muthafucka," he reminded her.

She laughed. "Reality check, nigga! It's in my name, so it's mine!"

"Bitch, I got something fo' ya," Lil Will threatened.

She hung up and said to herself, *I'm going to have his ass downtown if he comes here with that bullshit.* Then she had a second thought when the phone rang. "Hello," she said, answering the phone.

"Hey beautiful. It's me, Ju-Ju. I was thinking about you, so I decided to give you a call," he said.

"You so sweet, Ju-Ju. I wish all niggas could be this way," Monica said.

He noticed the sadness in her voice. "Why you sound sad, luv?"

"A lot on my mind," she said.

"I'm here if you want to talk about it," he said.

"Just got off the phone with Lil Will. He's on his way back to Boston. We had a fight over the phone. I'm scared and I don't know what to do," Monica told Ju-Ju.

"Do you need me to come get you?" he asked,

"I don't know. You don't know Lil Will. He's not to be fucked with," she said.

"So? I ain't scared of him. Nigga's heart pumps blood like mines," Ju-Ju said, feeling a little offended by her comment.

"Listen, Ju-Ju, Lil Will kill you and won't lose a second of sleep," she said.

"I ain't no saint, luv. When it comes down to it, he can be touched too. Just let me come get you or meet me somewhere and we can go from there," he said compromisingly.

Monica, being actually scared, said, "I don't think that's a good idea. I can't handle it if he finds out about you."

"Luv, let me worry about that. I tell you what. Just call me if things get out of hand," he told her.

"I will. I promise," she said.

"Goodnight, luv," Ju-Ju said.

"Goodnight, Ju-Ju," she responded.

They hung up. As the tears started to flow, Monica thought to herself, *What have I done?*

****

"Nigga, that's where that nigga Fred's mama lives," one of the gunmen said to Mark.

Mark was in the front van that circled around the block and parked on the back street. He had given orders for the second van to cover the front just in case Fred was inside and he tried to make a break.

As the four masked gunmen crept toward the house, Fred just so happened to be looking out of his bedroom window. "Fuck! How did they know I was here?"

He pulled a bag from under the bed. Thankfully, his parents weren't home. He pulled out two AKs and a Mack-11. Fred crept back to the window and opened fire on the first two men, catching one with a head shot. The other three gunmen dropped to the ground and fired back. Fred jumped behind the bed as bullets put holes in everything around him. Without second thought he dialed the one number he didn't want to.

"Nigga, pick up," he said heart about to beat out of his chest.

The phone rang two more times, but thankfully someone picked up. "Agent Scott speaking," the agent said, answering the phone.

"I need help! Niggas trying to kill me," Fred said, panicking. He jumped up, letting off a couple of rounds.

"Is that gunfire?" Agent Scott asked.

"Nah, it's fireworks," Fred said sarcastically.

"Where are you?" the agent asked.

"You know where a nigga at! Y'all keep tabs on me," Fred snapped.

"Listen, if you want my help, you got to answer my questions," Agent Scott said calmly.

"A'ight! A'ight! I'm at my mama's house," Fred yelled through the phone at the agent.

"Stay put. We got a team coming your way," said Agent Scott.

Fred hung up and prayed they'd be there soon.

"Man, jump the back gate, shoot up the back door, and kick it in," Fred heard one of the gunmen say to another.

"Fuck!" Fred screamed.

As he stood to go cover the rear, he got hit in the side. The impact sent him back to the wall, where he slid down to the floor. Blood was leaking to the floor from his right side. The pain was crucial. He tried to stand, but was on one knee when they cornered him. When he looked up, he was looking down the barrel of a gun. That alone told him it was his last day on earth.

"Drop the gun, Fred," demanded one of the masked gunmen.

He complied. They rushed him and took him out the back door because they knew it wouldn't be long before the police came. They put him in the van and turned off the street as three patrol cars passed them. The masked man in the back check Fred over.

"You'll live." The man looked at the blood soaking through the shirt. "It's just a flesh wound." He flipped open his phone and made a call. "We got him. He put up a fight and he got shot in the side. It's only a flesh wound. The bullet went through."

He hung up the phone and tapped the back of the driver's seat.

"Yeah," the driver said.

"Plan B. The meat store," said the gunman.

The rest of the ride was quiet. Fred had no idea where he was being taken, but somehow knew it wasn't looking good for him *Lord, what have I done?* he thought to himself.

Being in and out of consciousness, he hadn't realized that they stopped until the side door opened and he was being pulled out. They dragged him down a long dark hallway. One of the gunmen opened the door of a side room.

"Sit his bitch ass over there and tie him up," he heard a man say.

"What the fuck, bruh?" Fred asked out of fear. "What y'all want?"

One of the gunmen hit him in the head with the butt of the gun and said, "Shut the fuck up."

His mind went blank and black. They finished tying him up and the gunmen exited the room, locking the door behind them.

****

FBI Agent Scott entered Fred's parents' house. There were bullet holes everywhere to match the shell casings outside. He looked in every room, but no Fred to be found. He put in for an APB for Fred Johnson.

"Listen. Go door to door and see if anyone saw or heard anything that might give us a lead to Mr. Johnson's whereabouts. Let's get to work," Agent Scott said.

He had a hunch Fred was already dead, something he hoped he was wrong about because this was his star witness. Without him, he had no case against Lil Will.

"Fuck!" he yelled back in his car.

Agent Scott got back to the office and called a meeting. In his mind, it was time to pay Lil Will a visit. He posted several pictures of him on the bulletin board, mugshots and all.

"Okay everybody, listen up! This is Lil Will! That's his alias! I've been working this case for two years now, and he just got out after serving fifteen years upstate! This kingpin runs Boston down to Florida. Drugs and gun trafficking, you name it! We haven't been able to pinpoint his moves. Fred Johnson is my informant! His house was shot up tonight and we had to take his family to a secure location! We need to find out who's responsible and bring them in"

Everybody stood to leave. Agents Scott, Dunlap, and Wright stayed behind.

"Agent Scott," Agent Wright called out.

"What do you have, Agent Wright?" asked Agent Scott.

"I might know somebody who can shed some light on this case," Agent Wright said with confidence.

"Really? Why are you so late in telling me this?" Scott asked, shocked.

"Yes sir, I do know someone; however, they are my confidential informant," she replied.

"So, who is it?" asked Agent Scott.

"Again, Agent Scott, my confidential informant. Unless there is a deal on the table, I can tell you now that he will not talk. Meet me at the county jail tomorrow at nine," she told him.

"Okay," he said.

The next morning Agent Scott strolled in the county jail looking all business, but he was smiling inside when he met Agent Wright. They shook hands.

"Good morning, Agent Scott," she said warmly.

"Good morning," he replied. "Let's see if your source will give us something so we can put Lil Will away for life."

They walked into the holding cell, where the inmate was already sitting. Agent Wright introduced the two men to each other. "Agent Scott, this is Montana. Montana, this is my boss."

Montana was a hustler/killer who had worked for several mob bosses. That included Lil Will. He was doing fed time for moving so much coke that it made the newspaper reporters call him The Snowman. He'd pled guilty to the drug charges just to keep them off his ass about the unsolved murders that they were investigating him for playing a major part in.

After serving a good five years, Agent Wright had dug up enough dirt on him to pin the murders on Montana. His only way out of life in the feds was to become an outstanding snitch for her when his services were needed. Now Montana's services were needed, and she was there to cash in.

"Fuck that," Montana said. "Where the paperwork?"

Agent Scott acted like he didn't hear what Montana said. "What can you tell us about Lil Will?"

"I ain't sayin' shit 'til I get my deal," was Montana's response.

Agent Scott lost his cool. He grabbed Montana by the back of the head and slammed his face into the table, causing him to yell from the pain.

"Listen. I do not have time for game," the agent said coldly.

"Man, fuck you," Montana snapped. "You don't know this nigga too well. I need my family safe, then I'll talk. But I ain't saying anything until that's done."

He told Agent Wright to go get the paperwork.

"Now let's talk," he said, turning his attention back to Montana.

Montana laughed as he spoke. "Well, Willie James, a.k.a. Lil Will, is bigger than you think. He runs the entire east coast. He is Mr. Cartel himself. The nigga got everybody on his payroll. Not to mention, he got some real killas on his team."

"Have you seen someone kill for him?" asked Scott.

"Yeah," he replied.

"Were you with them, or were you one of the killers?" Scott asked.

"All of the above," Montana said.

"How many bodies?" Scott asked Montana.

"15, 20...hell, I don't know. I lost count," Montana answered.

Agent Scott was satisfied with his answers. "Good man," he said to Montana. "Agent Wright, have him processed out and moved to the safest federal prison in this fucking country."

"Already on it, sir," she told him.

"What about my family?" asked Montana.

She gave him a thumbs up. "Already on that too, Montana."

Agent Scott shook hands with him and walked out smiling. *Got that ass now, Lil Will*, he thought to himself.

Chapter Nine

Monica found herself at Ju-Ju's apartment. She nodded her head as she admired his taste. "This you?" she asked admiringly.

"Yeah. This is my place - and yours, if you'd like to stay," he replied genuinely.

"Okay. Okay. I see you got some flava 'bout ya self," Monica said comically.

"Have a seat. You want something to drink? I got Ciroc and cranberry," he added. "Sure. That will be fine," she said as she sat down on the couch and relaxed.

"I will be right back," he told her and stepped out of the living room.

She looked around the room. Some pictures stood out to her. There was something familiar about them. She just couldn't remember where she had seen the faces.

Ju-Ju came back in the living room carrying two glasses and handed one to Monica. "Here you go."

She took the glass. "Thanks."

The night was moving smoothly. They laughed, talked, and sipped. Before they knew it, they were past tipsy. Ju-Ju pulled her shoes off and begun rubbing on her feet.

"Damn, that feels so good," Monica said, leaning back on the couch.

"Really?" asked Ju-Ju seductively?

He pulled her leg up and placed kisses on it. She closed her eyes as he rubbed and kissed on her leg. His hands went up her dress. The heat he felt between her thighs told him everything he needed to know.

He slid two fingers inside of her and slowly stroked while they kissed. She slipped her arm through the dress top and bra straps, revealing her breasts. His hands immediately went to them, massaging them while tonguing her down.

He stood up and pulled his pants down. She smiled at his rock hard erection and opened her legs wider. He didn't hesitate to get inside of her, causing her to moan.

"Mmm...baby...Ju-Ju...fuck me, baby...yeah...just like that... Mmm. Ooooh. That dick good to me, baby!" she cried. She thrust her hips forward and tightened the inside of her sex around him while moaning in his ear. The shit had him hooked.

"Oh shit, baby! I'm 'bout to cum!" he yelled.

"Cum then, baby! Ooooh! Ooooh! Cum up in this good pussy!" she screamed. They both climaxed at the same time. She had never experienced anything like it.

"Oh my God. Damn, you know how to fuck, Ju-Ju," she said, breathing hard.

"You okay?" he asked. She was shaking uncontrollably.

"Yes! It's just been a long time since I been pleased with being pleased," she said with a smile.

Ju-Ju went to the bathroom and turned on the shower. While the water was heating up, she saw her phone light up with an unread text message. It was Lil Will.

"Shit!" she yelled.

Ju-Ju came running out of the bathroom. "What's good, luv?"

"Lil Will just texted me. He is in Boston," she said with fear vibrant in her words.

"And?" he replied, not the least bit worried.

"He said he had a run to make and afterward he will be home. Dammit!" she exclaimed.

"You know you don't have to leave," he said, voice calm but full of emotion.

"I know, Ju-Ju. You're sweet, but we moving too fast and I ain't trying to make no mistakes," she said with caution.

"I'm really feeling you, Monica. I can take care of you. I got money," he said.

"Money ain't shit if you dead," she said sarcastically.

"That nigga bleeds just like me," he snapped, feeling offended.

Monica knew then she had made a mistake. "I got to go," she said, getting up off the couch.

She straightened her dress back up and rushed home. When she got home, she damn near broke an ankle getting to the shower. It was the first time she had ever cheated on Lil Will. The loyal part of her heart knew she would tell him, but the logical side of how she was going to tell him wasn't so enthused.

****

Lil Will called a meeting at the pool hall. Just to look like a normal outing, they shot a few games of 8 ball and drank a few brews. They waited until no one was really paying attention to them before heading to the back room. Two by two they crept off from the pool table and into the back room.

"I got to say," Lil Will said, looking from hustler to hustler, "shit looking great for the team. Are the guys ready to sell?"

"Luck and Nard are, but John said no," one of the runners said.

"Well," Lil Will, said shaking his head, "we tried it the business way. Now we will do it our way. Send some shooters at him. If the nigga don't comply, rock his ass to sleep."

"Done," the runner said, getting on the phone.

"And send the money for the kids' playground to be built on 18th," Lil Will demanded. "Any news?"

"One of our men up top say we got a rat," another runner said.

"Find out who," Lil Will told him. "Anything else?"

Tony stood up. "I been following Monica like you told me. She been kicking it with a nigga from out of town."

Lil Will shook his and laughed. "Figures. Find out who this

nigga is and what he be about. Anything else? No? Good. I'm going home. Nigga tired as hell."

Everybody filed out of the room just as cautiously as they went it.

Lil Will pulled up at his crib. He sat in the truck talking to Mark on the phone for a minute. All the while he stared at the house. All the lights were out.

"Yo, you good, fam?" Mark asked?

"I'm good. Just tired as shit," Lil Will said.

"We will get up. Go get some rest, bruh," Mark said, concerned.

"Love, fam," Lil Will said and then hung up the phone.

He hopped out and made his way inside. He looked upstairs, but decided to crash on the sofa.

The hallway lights came on and Monica came downstairs. "Lil Will, is that you?" she asked.

"Yeah, it's me," he said tiredly. "Who the fuck else am I supposed to be? You expecting company?"

By the sound of his voice, she could tell something was wrong. She walked on down the stairs and stood next to the couch. "Are you okay?" she asked.

"Yeah," he replied, irritated. "I'm just sleepy. Long day."

She sat in the chair next to the couch. "Listen, Will, we need to talk about us."

"I'm all ears. Talk," he said.

"See," she said, feeling neglected, "this the shit I been talking about."

"Monica, if you brought yo' ass downstairs to argue," he said, frustrated, "save it."

"Just listen to what I got to say, Will," Monica said, her voice full of emotion.

His phone rang and he didn't hesitate to answer. "Talk to me."

"It's Mark, fam. I'm at yo' door. We got to take a ride," the caller said.

"I'm on my way," Lil Will said and then hung up the phone.

Furious, Monica said, "See, niggas like you make good women say fuck it!"

"What in the hell you talking about, Monica?" he yelled. "Your ass act like a nigga out here doing this shit for hisself! Bitch, you spend more of my money than I do, and you got fucking nerve to stand here bitching about quality time!"

"Nigga, money don't solve every gotdamn problem in the universe!" she yelled back. "I love you because of the nigga you was when I met you! But I see now money changes a nigga's emotions towards a bitch!"

"Man, I ain't got time for this shit," he said and then walked out.

As he left, she ran upstairs crying. She buried her face in the pillow. All she could think of was how big of a fool she had been thinking Lil Will really ever gave a damn about her. She cried herself to sleep.

****

Henry was in the tub. The steaming hot water was doing the trick. Finally he was relaxing, but his thoughts lingered on the edge of murder. *Mike has to die*, he thought to himself.

Sabrina walked in and said, "Can I join you?"

He looked up at the image of the goddess. There she was, naked, and looking real damn tasty. "By all means," he said.

She eased in the bath sideways and began massaging his sex until it was fully erect. He closed his eyes and sighed.

"You like that, daddy?" she said lustfully.

"Hell yeah," Henry replied.

She eased up and on to him backward and started slow grinding. She moaned and her body trembled from the stimulating length of him inside of her. He massaged her breasts and got into the groove with her grinding motion.

"Damn, girl, you feel so good inside," he said.

"Yes, baby," she said between moans.

She propped her legs up on the side of the tub and leaned back, letting her head rest on his shoulder. "Get this pussy, baby," she commanded.

He grabbed her under the thighs and started pounding up inside of her.

"Yeah, baby! Just like that! Oh my God," she screamed. She worked her muscles around him and met his thrusts with an equal amount of force.

"Yeah! Pound this pussy! You like the way I take that dick? Huh? Huh?" she screamed louder and louder.

"Oh shit! I'm 'bout to cum," he yelled.

The strokes got harder, faster, and shorter until he released. It was like all the pressure of the day was gone.

"Damn, Sabrina, you just made a fucked-up day end perfect," he said, breathing hard.

"Thank you and you're welcome. A bitch done did her job," she said.

They let the water drain out of the tub and took a shower together. Henry could not resist the urge to be inside of her again. He pinned her up against the wall underneath the running water and entered her from behind.

"Damn, baby," she said softly, "you can't get enough of this good pussy."

He responded by grinding harder, filling her up from behind. They climaxed together again. She turned around and kissed Henry on the lips before saying, "You must be trying to get a bitch pregnant?"

"I'm good with that too," he said.

After the shower, they laughed and kicked it until they fell asleep. The next morning, she woke him up with her lips wrapped firmly around his dick. He released and then she jumped up headed to the bathroom, where she got ready for work.

"Where you running off to this morning?" he yelled after her. "And what time is it anyway?"

"It's 7:45 and I got to clock in to get this check," Sabrina said as she walked back through the bedroom. "You okay this morning?"

"How can a man not be with a woman like you around?" he said.

"Great question. Anyway, what your day looking like?" she asked.

"Check up on my mama and business. You want to get up on your lunch break?" he asked.

"Sure. I'll call you around one," said Sabrina.

She walked out of the house feeling like a true breadwinner. She actually had a nigga with a good heart, a check, and some good dick, she thought to herself as she jumped in her Toyota Camry and drove off. She hit Sopia on speed dial.

"Hey bitch," Sopia answered, saying. "What you up to this morning?"

"Bitch," she replied jokingly, "I have been laid and slayed."

Sopia laughed. "Oh, you and Henry getting along just fine then. That's what's up."

"Yep," Sabrina said happily. "But a bitch got to play her cards right."

"You can say that again," Sopia replied. "That is that nigga's check. Bitch, you better keep your own well from running dry."

"And you know it," Sabrina shot back. "But I'm on my way to work. I'll get at you when I get off."

"Alright Sabrina," Sopia said and hung up.

Sabrina put her phone on the charger and Bluetooth the music to play through the car speakers as she drove to work.

****

Bee and Teddy watched as Mike pulled out of the projects.

"Bee, what the hell Mike doing over here?" asked Teddy curiously.

"Beats me. Let me hit this nigga up," Bee said and then he jumped on the phone. He called him.

"Hello," Mike answered.

"What's up, fam?" Bee said.

"Shit, chillin'. Getting my money up," Mike replied.

"Word," Bee said, watching him. "I feel that, my nigga."

"Yeah, you know me," Mike said.

"That's for real. Check game," Bee said. "Where you at?"

"On Corn at one of the spots," he lied.

"Yeah?" Bee said, heated.

Bee knew he was lying and it didn't sit too well with him. "Meet me about six on The Dark Side."

"Got you, Bee," Mike said.

They hung up. He couldn't believe this shit he'd just witnessed. "What he say?" Teddy asked.

"Bruh," Bee said, still in disbelief, "the nigga just lied. I don't know why."

"This Henry's zone. Something ain't right," Teddy said.

"Hell nah, it ain't," Bee said. "We need to find out before shit gets out of hand."

As they were talking, Henry hit Teddy's line.

"Talk to me," Teddy answered. "What's good with you?"

"A whole lot," Henry said. "I got to spend some time with my family. My pops died last night."

Teddy dropped his head. He hated to hear about a good nigga losing loved ones. "Damn, fam, my heart goes out to you and the family. If you need anything, just call. I got you, bruh."

"Alright," Henry said.

"One, fam," Teddy said. He hung up and shook his head.

"That was Henry. His pops passed last night."

"So he's with his family," Bee said.

"Yep," Teddy replied.

"Good," Bee said, a little relieved. "Let's make our rounds and get this money to the spot. And call Dink to see if he's ready so we can ship this money to Lil Will."

Teddy called Dink immediately. He answered his phone on the third ring. "Yeah," he said, sounding irritated. "What up, Teddy?"

"Just hitting you up to make sure everything is in order," said Teddy. "A nigga trying to keep shit together and on a consistent timeline."

"I understand that, bruh," said Dink, "but you still haven't said what the fuck you called me for."

Teddy held his temper. Dink definitely knew how to get up under a nigga's skin. He took a deep breath and said, "We collecting to ship out no later than tomorrow morning. Have the fucking money right."

Teddy hung up. He didn't want to hear the bullshit he knew was about to come out of his oldest brother's mouth.

"I swear if that nigga wasn't my mother and father's son," Teddy said still heated, "I would fuck his whole world up."

"You and everybody else," Bee said and laughed.

They pulled up on the Westside of Albany. Lil Nook and a couple of other niggas from the Westside Crew were out clocking dollars. Bee looked at them and shook his head and said to Teddy, "Man, I hope Lil Nook ain't on the fuck shit today."

Lil Nook was a real Westside nigga. Bee had a run-in with him a couple of years ago about a Westside hoodie he was knocking off for a while named Trisha. He had cut her off shortly after because she was the possessive type. Just so happened, Trisha was Lil Nook's sister.

He and Bee ended up knuckling up at The Fox. Bee had taxed his ass that night.

They swerved up on the curve in front of the trap house that

97

they had established on the Westside.

Bee cocked his .45 and checked the clip and concealed it under his shirt before he and Teddy got out. They noticed Lil Nook watched them the entire time. Don D was sitting on the front porch when they walked up.

"What up Teddy?" Don D said. "Bee?"

Don D was old school. He used to run with Big Will, Teddy, and Bee's pops back in the day. The word in the streets was Don D had fallen off, smoking the yams.

The two brothers nodded. Don D got up and walked inside the house and they followed behind him. Inside, they sat down on the sofa. Don D tossed Bee a half ounce of grass and two blunts and said, "Make yourself useful, young gangsta, while I grab the cake."

Bee sat back and started twisting up. He had finished twisting up all three blunts and Don D still hadn't shown back up. He began to get a bad feeling that some shit was about to go down.

"Teddy," he said while pulling out his strap, "check and see what that fool doing. It's been over twenty minutes. It don't take that long."

Teddy hopped up off the sofa. He cautiously made his way to the back room, trying his best not to make any noise just in case something was going down. When he peeped through the crack of the room door, he became pissed off. Don D had a crackhead sucking him off while he sucked on the glass dick.

Teddy eased back to the living room and motioned for Bee to follow him. They crept back to the back room and peeped through the crack. Seeing the pipe in Don D's mouth was more than Bee could handle. He kicked in the door with the gun aimed at Don D.

"Nigga, if you flinch wrong, I'm pushing your shit back," Bee said angrily. "Bitch, get up!"

The naked white lady got up off of her knees. The looks of her was disgusting. She was skinny, tall, and her breasts sagged damn near to her waist.

"Hold on, young gangsta," Don D pleaded. "I'm going to straighten it out. Give me a week."

He grabbed a brown paper bag from under the bed and tossed it to Teddy. "That's a little over half of the money right there. Trust me, I'm going to fix it. It's just that an OG be stressing sometimes, and a nigga need a quicker picker upper."

Bee's trigger finger was itching and Teddy knew it.

"Listen, Bee, if you twist this nigga's shit loose, you got to finish the job. No witnesses," Teddy said.

Bee responded by letting two rounds go into the woman's chest before walking up on Don D and dome calling him. Teddy hurried up and threw the rest of the product into a trash bag. On their way through the living room, Bee grabbed the blunts and weed, and they strolled out of the house like nothing had happened.

Willie Slaughter

Chapter Ten

Teddy, Bee, Mike, Dink and their main runners had counted the money they had collected. They put their cuts to the side and then put the re-up money inside two briefcases. Dink, his mind being everywhere but it should've been, hadn't paid attention to the count.

"Nigga, how much this is?" he asked Teddy.

"250 G's, Dink," Teddy said, frustrated. "Your ass would know if you would've been counting like everyone else."

Dink wanted to shoot back at him, but he let it slide. "Okay. Take that and this bag. It's 750 G's. Give it to bruh."

"Okay," Teddy said as he grabbed the duffle bag.

"I'll call him and let him know you on the way. I'm hitting 23rd and checking on this business I'm tryin' to buy," Dink said and then walked out.

As he drove off, Dink was thinking about his brother Lil Will and how he was back on top of the game. He himself was clocking a major check, but it wasn't shit compared to his brother's bank. It wasn't like he didn't know who the connect was.

As he thought about the shit, Dink got mad. In his mind, he was the oldest, so why was he taking orders instead of giving them?

At that thought his phone rang. It was his partner. "Yeah," Dink said.

"I got something good for you," the caller said. "You know where to meet me."

"Okay," Dink replied. "What time?"

"I will contact you when I get everything in order and let you know," the man on the other end of the line said.

"Good. We will get up," Dink said and then hung up.

A smile crept across his face. Instead of keeping to his route, he turned around and headed home. Everything was looking up for him so he thought, what better way to celebrate then digging off in some good pussy?

****

Lil Will and Mark walked through Platinum, which was one of the clubs Mark owned. When they reached the office, he noticed someone already sitting inside in his chair.

"What's up, Mark?" the lady sitting in his chair said.

Mark looked at Lil Will, who was looking at the lady, curious as to what she wanted. "You need to hear what she has to say," Mark told him. "Go ahead, Agent Wright."

She propped her feet up on his desk. "Well, your boy Montana jumped ship on you. He's a federal witness now. And boy, does my partner got a hard on for you."

"New York Montana?" asked Lil Will.

"Yep. And Fred," Agent Wright stated.

"So how bad is it? How much have they been talking?" Lil Will wanted to know.

"Enough to have your ass on canned goods for life plus another go around. Agent Scott is meeting with the judge tomorrow to bring charges on you and to have a warrant issued for your arrest," she said.

"Fuck! Where these cheese eating-ass niggas at?" Lil Will said, heated about the situation.

"Nobody knows where Fred is at," the agent said.

"What you mean nobody knows?" Lil Will asked, confused.

"Just like I said, nobody knows. And Montana is being transferred to a safe house tonight," Wright added.

"Shit! Get me the info. I'll handle it. I also need to pay Agent Scott a visit," he said nervously. Mark handed the agent a bag. "'Preciate the info."

Slaughter Gang

"No problem. I'll be sure to keep you informed," she said.

Agent Wright draped the bag across her shoulder and walked out. In the car sitting in the parking lot, she took out a micro-recorder and played the tape. After playing it three times, she edited it. In her mind it was like an insurance policy.

Inside the office, Lil Will was pacing the floor. "Fuck! Fuck! Fuck! This shit can't be happening. The cartel will stop the shipment if they hear about any of this shit."

"Listen, fam," Mark said. "Let me get the crew on the line to get this shit handled before sun up. You just go back to GA and lay low."

"I will, after I look that nigga Fred in the eyes before he drops," Lil Will said. "Also I got to make sure the shipment got through."

"Alright, fam," Mark said as his phone vibrated on his hip. He pulled out his phone. He had received a text message. Mark opened it and read it. "Dammit, man. We got Fred's ass."

"Where?" asked Lil Will.

"The Meat Shop on 6th Street," replied Mark.

"Let's go," Lil Will said.

On the way there they made sure that they weren't being followed. Mark parked around the back of the store. Four men carrying AK-47's met them in the hallway. One of them told them to follow him.

They entered the side room to see Fred chained to a steel chair in the center of the room. They had beat him just that bad. The gunmen left, leaving Lil Will and Mark with Fred to do as they pleased.

"My nigga, Fred Johnson," Lil Will said comically. "Rat-ass nigga."

"Man, I'm sorry," Fred said. Tears flowed freely from his eyes, mostly because of the fear of death, which in his mind at the time was better than what plans they might have.

"Why, Fred? A nigga ain't been good to ya?" Lil Will asked.

"The fed nigga Scott dropped in on me and fucked me over with some trumped-up shit he planted. Then he literally tortured my ass while threatening to put my ass away for a good thirty piece and having my pregnant girl locked up too," Fred said.

"Fo' what? Shit ain't making sense, Fred," Lil Will said.

"Nigga said it's personal between you and him," replied Fred.

"Personal how?" asked Lil Will.

"Some shit 'bout you killed his brother," Fred said. "Will, he made me say the shit that I said. I wasn't going to do it."

And those were his last words. Lil Will shot him four times in the face. They walked out and on the way back to their ride, he told the gunmen to make sure they swept the scene clean.

"So what now, fam?" Mark asked?

"We fuck Agent Scott's li'l world up," Lil replied.

Three navy blue and tinted windows jump out vans with an eight man crew in each cruised through the neighborhood where Agent Scott lived. When they pulled up in front of the house, two of the crews crept around back and the other three stayed out front with AR 15s with the hundred round drums.

With no warning, they opened fire on the house. Agent Scott was headed to the bathroom when the bullets whizzed by his head.

"Shit!" Scott yelled.

He dropped on the floor and crawled back into the bedroom, where he screamed at the sight of his wife sprawled across the bed with a hole in her head and chest and the bed linen soaked with her blood. He grabbed her lifeless body and held it close.

"I'm sorry, baby," he said in between sobs. "I'm so, so sorry." He laid her body down and closed her eyelids. Without a care in the world he grabbed his gun and ran to the living room window. "Y'all motherfuckers are dead!"

He put two slugs in the chest of the first gunman near the

window. He hit three more with straight head shots. He heard a sound coming from behind him but by the time he reacted, he took one in the left arm.

As he went down, he rolled behind the couch, out of the gunman's line of fire and reloaded. He waited patiently on the masked man to turn the corner, and when he did, Agent Scott let him have it. He heard doors slamming and tires screeching and knew the assault was over - at least, that was what he thought until he heard more gun shots.

Cautiously, he made his way over to a window and peeped out just in time to see the unmarked cars. It was a shootout. The agents in the first car got hit up bad, causing the other two cars to veer off course as it hit a fire hydrant. The other two cars got sprayed up so bad they were forced to stop their pursuit.

"Call for backup," Agent Scott yelled.

Agent Scott had come running down the street, unloading the clip at the vans. "Fuck! They got away," he said angrily as he walked back towards the house.

Police surrounded the house and radioed for the E.M.Ts to collect the dead. They asked him questions about what had happened. He gave them a full report, but all the while, his mind was on Lil Will. He couldn't prove it, but he knew he was behind this, and he would pay dearly for his wife's death.

****

Mark and Lil Will were on their way back to Lil Will's crib when the text came through Mark's phone, letting them know Agent Scott had survived, but his wife didn't. And he wanted blood for blood. Lil Will chuckled.

"So be it," he said.

"Nah, fam," Mark responded. "It's too hot up here. You need to fall back. Go lay low."

"After this meeting with the connect, I'm getting ghost," Lil Will promised.

"Good," Mark commented. "Because I can handle shit here. Be safe, my nigga."

"Yeah. Love, fam," Lil Will said.

He hopped out and made his way to the front door. He tried to unlock the door with his key, but it wouldn't turn. *I know this bitch didn't*, he thought to himself. "Monica!"

He banged on the door. She didn't open it; however, she opened the upstairs window and looked down at him.

"What you want?" she yelled.

"Bitch, you done went crazy," Lil Will said madly.

"Nah, nigga," she shot back, "yo' ass the one crazy if you think I'm going to keep playing this game with you!"

"Open my goddam door now, Monica," he yelled.

"Nigga, this my door and my house! Yo' name ain't even on the lease," she reminded him.

"Open this door, Monica! I ain't playin'," he said threateningly.

"No, Will! This shit all yo' fault! Please just leave," she begged.

"I'm going to fuck you up! I promise you! You and that nigga Ju-Ju! What, you think I didn't know, bitch?" he said, laughing.

Hearing his name made her adrenaline rush. She began to cry harder. She knew she loved Lil Will, however, his knowing about her and Ju-Ju meant it was over between them.

"Bitch, I'm gone, but I'll be back in the morning! Yo' ass better be gone or you a dead bitch," he threatened. He jumped in his ride and peeled off.

The next morning he met with the top dogs. They discussed future business, and money was exchanged for the unseen product, but a damn good profit. After the meeting, the head pulled him to the side.

"My man, I hear you having some problems," he said to Lil

Will.

"Nothing I'm not handling," Lil Will said reassuringly.

"Good, because I don't like problems. They bad for business. Especially this business," he said.

"I'll fix it," Lil Will said confidently.

"I'm sure you will. You will get the next shipment, but before anything else moves, clean up your mess," he said.

Without waiting for a response, he walked off, followed by two bodyguards.

Lil Will left and stopped at his club, where he found Mark.

"Yo Mark," he said to get his attention, "get some guys over to the warehouse and wait on the shipment."

"Got you. What's on yo' mind?" asked Mark.

"Not too much of anything good at the moment. Just got to tie up some loose ends. I'll meet you at the airport at 6:00," Lil Will said.

"Alright, fam. Be careful. You know the alphabet boys watching," Mark reminded him.

They went their separate ways. Lil Will needed answers fast. He knew where Rimp was being held and that's where he went. As soon as Rimp saw him, he asked him what was up.

"Cut him loose," Lil Will told one of the guys keeping Rimp hostage.

They untied him and stepped back. Rimp stretched and rubbed his wrists. "Fam, what's this shit all about?" Rimp demanded to know.

"I had to find out who was working fo' the people," Lil Will replied.

"My nigga, you know it's death before dishonor with me," Rimp said defensively. "As long as we have been doing this shit together, bruh!"

"I know, fam," Lil Will said, "but guess who the rat was? Fred."

Rimp frowned. "You bullshitting."

"Nigga went fed on me. Nigga been squealing. Sang a song

that cost a nigga 680 months," Lil Will said.

"Where this nigga at?" Rimp asked.

"Listen. You a free man. Get ya shit straight and holla back at me. Matter of fact, I got to take a trip. Mark will be holding shit down," Lil Will said.

He left. When he got to the house, the door was unlocked and Monica was gone. He searched the house and realized all of her personal belongings were gone. He checked the wall safe. All of his money was still there.

Trifling-ass bitch, he thought to himself. He knew she was with Ju-Ju. He scrolled through his contacts to find her friend's Erica number and called. "Erica, this Lil Will," he said.

"Oh, hi," Erica said.

"Don't play games with me. Where Monica?" he asked.

"I don't know. I haven't talked to her," Erica replied.

"I know you know. And I know you know 'bout her and the nigga from out of town. When I find out, I'm killing you all," Lil Will threatened.

He hung up. Not trying to waste any time, he packed a few outfits and left. While pulling off from the curb, he called Mark.

"A nigga tired. What's up?" Mark said.

"Find Monica and put her ass to sleep with that nigga Ju-Ju," Lil Will ordered.

At the mentioning of that name, Mark became fully awake. "Ju-Ju?" he said.

"You heard me. The bitch been creeping with him while we were handling business," Lil Will stressed.

"Ju-Ju from Lynn, Mass?" Mark asked.

"I think so. Do you know the nigga?" Lil Will asked.

"If it's the Ju-Ju I know, he's Snake brother," Mark explained.

"I'll be damned. Lil Ju-Ju. So he tryin' to take my bitch. Pick a plot fo' his ass next to her," Lil Will said.

"So be it, fam. I'm on it," said Mark.

After they ended the conversation Lil Will called to GA. "What's up, Teddy?" Lil Will said.

"What's good?" Teddy replied.

"Did you all get that," Lil Will asked?

"Yeah," said Teddy

"Good. I'm on my way. Too hot up here. Y'all be on standby," Lil Will said.

"Bet," Teddy replied and then hung up.

Headed down 5th and 9th to the airport, Lil Will was so deep in thought he didn't see the fed car tailing him until it was too late. They pulled up beside him with flashing lights and with their badges on display, telling him to pull over.

"Fuck," he said to himself. He pulled out his cell phone and called his lawyer. He picked up just as the agents approached with guns drawn.

"Get out the car now! Or we will be forced to shoot to kill," the lead agent yelled.

He opened the door and got out with his hands above his head. That didn't stop them from getting a little rec off him. They roughed him up a little before and after cuffing him. Due to the fact his lawyer was still on the phone, he smiled as they put him in the backseat.

His lawyer, after overhearing and recording the matter, started making calls to see where his client was being taken, but it was too early to find the information he needed.

"Okay, thank you. I'll call back tomorrow morning," the attorney said and then hung up.

Lil Will was transported to Florida. Agent Scott, upon seeing him, didn't think twice. He punched him in the face until he got tired. Lil Will spat blood on the floor.

"Damn. You feel better now? How does it feel to hit a real nigga?" Lil Will teased.

"You fucked up, my man. Do you know who I am?" Scott asked threateningly.

"Yeah," Lil Will laughed. "A fuckin' nobody to me."

"You killed my wife, and you, my man, are going to pay," Agent Scott said.

"What the hell? I ain't killed nobody," Lil Will said, offended.

"I know you sent your boys to kill me, but as you can see, I'm still here. But my wife didn't make it," the agent said, fighting back the emotion.

"Man, I don't know what the fuck you talking 'bout," Lil Will proclaimed.

"I'm pretty sure you killed Fred Johnson too. He's missing," Scott said.

"I don't know no Fred," Lil Will said.

"Well, we will see about that," the agent said confidently.

"I want to call my lawyer. Until then, I have nothing to say to you," Lil Will said, knowing his rights.

The door opened. An agent walked in followed by a slim fine black woman in a beige pants business suit.

Agent Scott eyed her. "May I help you?"

"Yes you can," she said while producing her credentials. "I'm with the law firm and an associate of Willie James's lawyer."

Agent Scott's heart skipped a beat. "Come again?"

"I'm here on the behalf of Willie James, a client of the law firm I work for. I would like to know how his face got like this," she added.

"In an attempt to elude my fellow agents, he hit a tree," Agent Scott said.

"Oh, really?" she replied.

The agent who had accompanied her took the cuffs off of him.

"To be clear, I'll be filing a suit against the agency," she threatened.

They left. As they walked through the parking lot, she asked him if he was okay.

"Yeah, but how did you find me so fast?" he asked.

"Your phone. G.P.S.," she answered.

"Thanks, Mrs. Knight," he said.

"Nigga, I ain't no Mrs. And call me Cynthia," she said sarcastically.

"Okay, Cynthia. Let's get the hell away from here," Lil Will said.

Agent Scott was heated. Inside of the interrogation room, he flipped over the table and threw the chairs against the wall. Under his breath he swore to kill him. What the hell was the foolproof plan? As he thought about it, a smile spread across his face. *I got you. We'll play by your rules, Lil Will*, he thought to himself as he walked out of the room on the phone.

Willie Slaughter

Chapter Eleven

The head of the cartel was eating grapes in the study at his estate. He was 5'9" with a short cropped hair cut, a medium built Italian. He had been running the illegal business of drug trafficking for the past forty plus years.

"Sir, you sent for me?" the butler asked.

"Yes. Bring me the phone," the head of the cartel commanded.

"Yes sir," the butler said.

The butler came back and handed him the phone on a platter. He called to the States. His right hand man JC answered.

"Yes sir," answered JC.

"I got a call last night. Lil Will got picked up," he informed him.

"Yes sir, but he's out. His lawyer sprung him. Agent Scott wants him bad," JC added.

"This is bad for business," the head said.

"I know, sir. What do you want me to do?" JC asked.

"Nothing for now. Just keep tabs on him. Make sure no heat comes my way. If need be, take the agent out," he responded.

"Yes sir," JC said.

The call ended. He leaned back in his chair, thinking. He liked Lil Will. He looked at him like a son. The past year he'd made him a lot of money. He couldn't think of why the agent was gunning for Lil Will so hard, but he was bound to find out. He clicked a button on the desk. The butler walked back in the study.

"Yes sir," he said.

"Call Agent Johnson and let him know it's imperative that we meet by tomorrow morning. I'll be in Texas," he ordered.

"Yes sir," he said.

The head of the estate continued to eat his fruit. The thought of being undermined by a federal agent who was out for revenge on one of the best employees he had wasn't sitting too well with him. He ate the grapes one at a time while pre-planning the outcome he was going to make happen for Lil Will.

The butler reentered the room and announced that the chopper was ready to go. He thanked him politely for his assistance before getting up out of the chair. The butler escorted him to the waiting helicopter and told him to have a safe trip.

When he landed in Texas, armed guards were waiting on standby to escort him to the estate. On the way there, one of the armed men asked him if he needed to see Agent Johnson right away.

"No. I need to get a little rest. Just let him know I'm here," he replied.

"Yes sir. The Mexican's shipment is ready too, sir," the guard informed.

"Good. Make sure it's a go for the G.G.B. and Dell," the head ordered.

"Who's that?" the guard wanted to know.

"Me and his father go way back. He reached out to me about three months ago. I'll let him know to meet you tonight," answered the head.

"Yes sir," the guard replied.

They walked into the main building of the compound. An armed guard was on post every so many feet away. Each one snapped to attention and saluted him. He acknowledged them all by a wave of his left hand and nod of the head.

"No visitors until I notify you saying otherwise. Understood?" he asked the butler.

"Very much so, sir," replied the butler. "Would you care for anything to eat or drink?"

"No thank you," was his reply, "but thanks all the same. I only require a moment to rest before business comes."

"As you wish, sir," said the butler before leaving him to get settled in.

The head walked into the master bedroom. He took one good look at the king-sized bed and found himself laying in it. He was tired - not physically, but mentally drained from having to deal with the pros and cons of the life he lived.

He hadn't always been in the position he was in. And it was his always acknowledging the sacrifices and other things that he had done to get to this point that kept him making the best decisions for business.

****

Bee had personally driven to Dink's crib to see what was up and to give the layout of his plans.

"Bee, fuck that," Dink said defiantly. "I'm on my way and I do shit on my own time."

"Bruh, why you always got to make shit so difficult? Let's just make this money. We have a meeting in Miami where we're bringing in a couple hundred thousand or maybe a full million, so chill. Lil Will just copped what we need. You ready?" asked Bee,

"Yeah, I'm in," Dink replied.

"Good. Let's get this paper. Slaughter Boyz fo' life," said Bee.

Bee's phone rang. He pulled it out of the casing on his hip and answered. "Talk to me." It was Teddy.

"Is the nigga thinking straight today?" asked Teddy.

Bee couldn't help but laugh. "Yeah. He's in."

"Good. We need Dink on the team," Teddy said.

"Fo' sho'. The only thing Lil Will is concerned about is us payin' our dues to the Circle," Bee reminded him.

"Good. Let's do it," Teddy said, motivated.

Bee hung up with a smile on his face. Although he had told himself he would never fuck with Trisha's possessive ass again, he found his thoughts leaning towards swinging her way. Waiting on Dink to come back out of the house and fire up, he hit her line.

"What's good, bae?" Trisha said as she answered the phone.

Damn. It was almost like she was waiting on the phone to ring, Bee thought. "You, with your extra lip grip," Bee replied. "What are you doing for it, li'l lady?"

She paused for a minute, thinking about whether or not she should entertain the idea that was vivid within her mind. "I am not going to say what I want to say, bae."

Bee chuckled. "Why not? The world belongs to you. I'm just one of your number one fans who's trying to work myself into being your favorite."

"Whatever, nigga. What's on your mind though?" she asked knowingly.

"Us for another tryout," he said. "You game?"

"When?" she asked.

"In a few. Just keep that good-good on standby for me," he said.

He hung up just as Dink returned with a blunt already twisted. They burnt one together before Bee left.

****

After six months of being back in Albany, everything was going as planned for Lil Will. His brothers and The S.M.F. Crew had pocketed over a half million each. He, himself, had tripled his profit.

Teddy strolled in the office followed by Bee, who said, "What's good, bruh?"

"Chilling. Tryin to buy this new spot for us," Lil Will said.

"Where at?" Bee asked?

"Up town. The Old J.C. Penney's building," answered Lil Will.

116

Bee thought about the size of the place. "Damn, bro, what we going to do with that?"

"What you mean? Nigga, if I land the deal, that'll be the biggest club in Southwest," Lil Will replied.

"Anyway, Dink on his way with the money," said Bee.

"That's what's up, Bee. I got to fly out to Texas. The connect going to be there. We got to supply every damn city and county all the way down to South Florida by Monday," he said, sounding tired.

"Dammit, man," Teddy cut in on the conversation. "I talked with the Columbian earlier."

"Great. What's on their menu, Teddy?" asked Lil Will.

"Oh, they ready," Teddy replied.

"Make it do what it do. Shit, that's another four million a month," Lil Will calculated. Teddy and Bee rubbed their palms together, grinning.

"That's the move, bruh," Bee said.

"Y'all niggas want to hit the club scene before a nigga bounces?" Lil Will asked his brothers.

"Shit, let's do it," Teddy agreed.

They went to the Fox. Teddy, Bee, and Lil Will hadn't been inside a good ten minutes when Lil Will saw the same dark-skinned sister he bumped into the last time he was there.

He tapped Bee on the shoulder. "Aye, bruh. Look at the pretty motherfucker there," Lil Will said, hyped up.

"Do what you do, bruh," Bee said.

Lil Will strolled out of VIP onto the dance floor and purposefully bumped into her this time.

"Nigga, what's your problem?" she asked, irritated.

"Do you know me?" he asked.

"No," was her response, "and I really don't give a fuck to know."

"Hold up, Miss Lady! My name Lil Will," he added.

"And? Is that supposed to mean something to me?" she said sarcastically.

"Apparently not! Listen, let me buy you a drink! Get to know each other," he pleaded.

"I'll take it as your apology," she said.

"Come on," he said. He led her over to VIP, where he ordered five bottles of cranberry vodka and two bottles of Ciroc.

"So Miss Lady, what's your name?" he asked.

"Machumu," she said.

"What kind of name is that?" Lil Will wanted to know.

"The kind that only three people have," she said defensively.

"Okay. Okay. So what is it you do?" he asked, trying to get a hold of the situation.

"I'm a cook. I work at the Carter's Grill," she responded.

"Stop lying. I eat there all the time, and not once have I seen you," he snapped.

"No lie. Just like you will rarely catch me inside a club. It's not my cup of tea," Machumu said.

The more small talk they made, the more he realized he was very interested in knowing her for real.

"What about you? What's your story?" Machumu asked.

"What do you want to know?" he asked.

"Anything. Entertain me," she said, propping her arm up on the table.

"Let's see. I'm originally from Albany, but I moved to Boston. I'm about my business and I'm tryin' to be a boss," he replied.

"A boss at what?" she asked.

"Owning my own everything," he stated.

"Oh, I see. You a drug dealer," she said.

"No. I'm a businessman up top and down here," he said again.

"So you want it all?" Machumu asked.

"Why not?" replied Lil Will.

They were halfway through the third bottle and they were feeling it. She excused herself to the bathroom. While she was gone, his phone vibrated on his hip. He didn't answer the first two times, but they kept calling. *Who the fuck is this!* he thought to himself as he answered, "Hello?"

"Nigga, you a dead man," was all the male's voice said before hanging up the phone.

The line went dead. He put the phone down and watched Machumu walk through the crowd his way. When she reached the VIP booth, a gunshot echoed inside the club.

"Damn!" Lil Will yelled.

Everybody scrammed for the nearest exit. Lil Will and his brothers went out the side door, hopped in the ride, and burnt rubber getting somewhere. Bee pounded his fist against the steering wheel.

"Them li'l niggas be wilding in The Fox. Almost fucked up a good thing. I got this bitch I been slaying. I'm about to swing by her crib," Bee said.

"That's what's up, bruh. Just drop us off at the office. I got some calls to make," said Lil Will.

****

Monica and Erica were at Ju-Ju's spot chilling. She had come by to check on her since she hadn't talk to her friend in a while.

"Girl, it's been almost a year and yo' ass been caged in," Erica said. "Look at you. Head and nails all fucked up. Bitch, you need a makeover. That nigga Lil Will down in Georgia doing whatever the hell he chooses to do. I guarantee you that he is not giving a damn about you and living the good life."

"I know. I just feel so bad. I fucked up," Monica tried explaining. She started crying all over again.

"Nah, bitch," Erica warned, "we are not doing the guilt trip shit. Pep up, bitch. You got Ju-Ju on ya team."

"You right. But since we been together, his time limited,"

Monica replied.

"Girl, you know how niggas get when it comes to the money. The sex hasn't changed, has it" she asked.

"Nah, that nigga still dicking me down proper," Monica said. They laughed, high fiving.

"Monica, it's going to be okay," Erica said soothingly.

"I hope so," Monica replied.

"Where the nigga at anyway?" Erica asked.

"I think him and Tee somewhere in Jacksonville, Florida," said Monica.

"And he didn't tell me?" Erica snapped. Wait 'til Tee gets back. I'm going to fix his ass. Let's go get something to eat."

"Okay," Monica replied, feeling a little better.

They left the house. The guy keeping tabs on Erica immediately noticed the woman he was getting paid to find. But to be sure, he looked back at the picture his employer had sent to his phone. "Bingo," he thought out loud to himself. He could kill two birds with one stone.

It was an easy task. He would do the job, collect his money, and go home. He texted the number of his employer, who immediately called him.

"You got the go ahead," the voice on the phone confirmed.

Without hanging up the first phone, he picked up another. He had wired bombs to both cars, however, each car had a certain code he had to text for the bomb to explode. He watched them get into Erica's car and he waited for them to pull off the curb before he punched in a code on the dial pad. When he pressed send, the car exploded and fire and smoke filled the air.

"It's done," he said to his employer.

"Good. I'll meet you in an hour," the employer said.

Mark hung up and called Lil Will informing him on the job. "Yeah, it's done."

"What about Ju-Ju?" Lil Will asked immediately.

"Nobody seen him," Mark replied.

"Keep looking," Lil Will said, desperate to find Ju-Ju, "and remember, we need him alive. I also need you to meet me in California this weekend."

"Alright, fam," Mark said.

"Love, fam," Lil Will said and hung up.

Mark was missing his partner, but he knew it was still hot in Boston, and some of the shit still being done only made it hotter. He went over to the Eastside to check on business.

"Pete, what's good?" Mark asked as he pulled up on him with the passenger side window rolled down.

"Chilling, bruh. I got that for ya. Let me grab it out the back real quick," Pete said and then stepped into the house.

Mark parked on the curb and got out. He sat in the living room on the couch, waiting for Pete to bring the package. Pete walked back in carrying a duffle bag and handed it to him.

"Here you go," Pete said. "By the way, my people know that nigga Ju-Ju you was asking me 'bout. His brother Snake out of Lynn, Mass. You heard me, fam?"

"Yeah, I hear ya," Mark said quickly, still in deep thought.

So that's where I know him from, Mark thought to himself before saying, "Good looking out, Pete."

He left. Mark stopped at the sports bar to get a drink. He only planned to sit there for an hour, but his mind was so fucked up he ended up staying five. He had to find Ju-Ju quickly.

The nigga had gotten bigger and was bloodthirsty. Not to mention his other brother he knew worked for the feds.

"Oh shit," Mark said as it hit him.

It all made sense to him now. Mark jumped up and hurried out the door. He had to fill his partner in on the info he'd just received.

Willie Slaughter

Chapter Twelve

Sabrina was lounging on the couch reading *Pleasures* when Henry walked in. He hadn't been home a good two hours a day for the past three months. The shit was taking its toll on her.

"And where have you been lately?" she asked comically.

"Damn," Henry said annoyed. "I've been catching up on my business. Why?"

"I've been calling yo' ass 'round the clock. You never answer or return my calls. You didn't even think to text a bitch," Sabrina snapped.

"I didn't come here for this shit. Look, Sabrina, you know I just lost my pops and a lot of fucked up shit been happening," said Henry.

"Yeah, I know," she said quickly, "but I ain't one of them slow bitches either."

"That's a plus," he shot back sarcastically. "Go cook a nigga something to eat." He slapped her on the ass as she walked by, headed to the kitchen.

In the kitchen, Sabrina looked through the fridge until she found something to cook that she wanted to eat. Henry's sudden mood changes were getting a little irritating to her. *It's a good thing I still work and pay the apartment bills because this shit here is not what I was thinking,* she thought to herself. She took out some frozen chicken wings and set the pack in some hot water to thaw out.

****

"Damn, Tee," said Ju-Ju, "where these niggas at?"

"I called them earlier. They should be pulling up any minute," Tee assured him.

"I hope so. We need this work. I want to put it down on the Eastside first. That's the nigga's number one money maker. If we hit his pockets hard enough, he will pop up and I'll lay his ass down," Ju-Ju said confidently.

As they talked, a black Lexus XL pulled up. Four men got out and posted up on the hood of the car. Ju-Ju and Tee hopped out of their ride and stood by the hood of their ride.

"Just chill, Ju-Ju. Let me do the talking," Tee said before he looked one of the men in the eyes and said, "What up?"

"Money," the other man replied.

"All the time. Let me see what you got," said Tee.

One of the men went to the car, grabbed the backpack, and set it on the hood.

Tee and Ju-Ju walked over and viewed the product, which was five bricks of uncut. Ju-Ju tested it and nodded. Tee handed over the briefcase with the money in it.

"It's all there. We'll be back in a week," responded Tee.

"Cool. I'll let David know," he said.

"Hell, I was planning on calling him myself," said Tee.

They went their separate ways. Ju-Ju and Tee hopped back in their ride.

"Ju-Ju, we about to light the streets up with this shit," said Tee.

Ju-Ju nodded, his mind really somewhere else. "I know. That's the plan."

Ju-Ju's phone started ringing. He looked at the caller ID. It was his brother. "What the fuck this nigga want?" He answered the phone. "Yeah?"

"Where you at?" asked his brother.

"Heading out of Florida. Why?" asked Ju-Ju.

"Just get your ass back here now. We need to talk. Better yet, I'll meet you in New York tomorrow night," said his brother.

"A'ight," said Ju-Ju and hung up.

Ju-Ju knew something wasn't right. His brother never

called him making demands.

"Who was that?" asked Tee.

"Scott," replied Ju-Ju.

Tee had never really liked Ju-Ju's brother. Nothing personal. It was just the fact that he was a federal agent. A crooked-ass agent, at that. "What the hell he want?"

Ju-Ju hunched his shoulders. "Don't know. All he said is he wants to meet in New York tomorrow night."

Tee shook his head. He never trusted anyone who worked for the law enforcement, no matter who their family members were. "My nigga, I ain't even going to sugarcoat it. I don't trust your brother."

"Hell, I don't either, for that matter. But I know he got good intentions. He's on the same shit we on right now," said Ju-Ju.

"Oh shit," laughed Tee. "Scott want to get at the nigga Lil Will."

Ju-Ju nodded. "Yep. Nine times out of ten, that's probably what he wants to meet with us about."

"I might like your brother after all," said Tee.

They got off on the next exit. Ju-Ju was in deep thought. Only thing going through his mind was the memory of Lil Will killing his brother Snake. Ju-Ju was the youngest of the three.

Lil Will had smoked his oldest brother in broad daylight over a misunderstanding about business, some shit that Snake didn't have anything to do with. But, Ju-Ju thought to himself, the time had come for him to face the consequences for his actions.

****

Sopia was chilling at home. It was a day off, and she had plans on how she was going to enjoy it. As she rolled up a

125

blunt, a knock came at the front door. She rushed to see who it was.

She opened the front door to see Kerria. Sopia couldn't help but smile. She grabbed her friend and hugged her. "Girl, how you been?"

Kerria hugged her back. "I have been great, actually. It's been a minute, huh?"

Sopia nodded. "Yep. Come in."

Kerria stepped into the apartment and sat in the living room on the couch. Sopia handed her the blunt and a lighter.

"So what's been going on? Fill me in on the tea," Sopia said.

Kerria fired up the blunt. "Well, I've moved to Atlanta. Got a job clocking 80 G's a year."

"For real?" Sopia said.

Kerria hit the blunt and passed it to her. "Yep, and I'm dating a doctor."

Sopia hit the blunt twice and passed it back to her. "Get the fuck out of here!"

"That's what I'm trying to get yo' ass to do," Kerria said before hitting the blunt.

Sopia laughed. "Bitch, you know I'm happy fo' you!"

Kerria hit the blunt again and passed it back to Sopia. "Thanks. How about you, girl? What's been happening in the Good Life City?"

Sopia hit the blunt and choked. "Same shit," she said in between coughs. "Living from paycheck to paycheck. Trying to see what it's going to be with Lil Will and me."

"Sopia, don't tell me you still waiting on that nigga?" asked Kerria.

"Yes I am," replied Sopia.

Kerria ducked the blunt out. "Where he at?"

"From what I hear, he's down here. I haven't seen him though," said Sopia.

"Look, sis," Kerria said, grabbing her hand, "you need better and you can dam sho' do better. Come on to Atlanta with me."

She snatched her hand away. "Bitch, please. I'm staying right here."

Kerria threw her hands up in the air out of frustration. "Fine by me. But bitch, don't come calling me later crying with a sob-ass story."

Sopia laughed. "Girl, please. I appreciate the offer though, Kerria. You're a true friend."

Kerria hugged her. "I got to get the hell on. You need me, call me. I'm here."

Sopia walked her friend to the door. "Thanks for dropping by, homegirl."

Kerria threw up the peace sign and walked out to her new 500 Benz and left.

****

As Bee was looking for a parking spot at the mall, he noticed his girl hadn't been being herself lately.

"What's up with you?" he asked.

"Nothing. I'm good," she replied.

He looked at her out of the corner of his right eye. "Girl, you know I know you lying."

"You might get mad if I told you," was her response.

Bee frowned. "Why would you think that?"

She turned, looking out the window. "I'm pregnant."

His eyes got big. "When? I mean, how long?"

"I'm four months," she said.

Bee was excited. "Ah, man! Dee, you okay? What you need? Are you sick?"

She smiled, seeing how happy and excited he was.

"I'm 'bout to be a father! Yes! I got to call my mama," he went on.

Dee laughed. "Damn, boy, chill."

He got control of himself. "We going shopping fo' the baby too. What we having?"

She shrugged her shoulders. "I don't know yet."

He grabbed her hand. "Whatever you want or need, I got you."

She smiled. "Okay, baby. I love you, Bee."

He grabbed her hand with his free hand. "I love you too, Dee."

Bee drove around until he found a suitable parking spot. Since the news he had just got about Dee being pregnant, he was taking all precautions. After making three rounds around the parking lot, someone was finally pulling out of a parking space close to the entrance of the mall. Bee parked and they got out and walked hand in hand into the mall.

They literally shopped until they dropped. They hit every children's store in the mall. Between the things he bought for their unborn child and Dee, he spent forty thousand with ease. She was tired and hungry by the time they reached the car.

"Baby, can we please stop to get something to eat," Dee said while rubbing her stomach.

He finished putting the bags in the back seat and jumped behind the wheel. "No problem."

They stopped by Wendy's and she ate enough for the both of them. She fell asleep when they got back in the car. On their way home, Teddy called.

Bee answered. "What up, bro?"

"I need you to meet me on 10th. Now," Teddy said in a serious tone.

Bee looked over at Dee, who was sound asleep. "A'ight. Let me drop Dee off."

"One," Teddy replied and hung up.

As Bee hung up, she looked at him. "Damn. So you just going to drop me off? I thought this was our day?"

He sighed. "Dee, please don't start. If you enjoy the money, you got to accept what comes with it. Come on. I'll be back soon."

She turned to stare out of the window. "Fuck you. Just take me home."

He dropped her off and carried the bags in the house. "Look, it won't take me long. Just chill."

Dee started unpacking and putting things away. "Bye, Bee."

He left, making his way to 10th Street, where they had a safe house nobody knew about but him and Teddy. He walked in on Teddy twisting up a blunt. He pounded Teddy up. "What up, bruh?"

Teddy fired up the blunt and passed it to Bee. "We got a problem. Got a call saying one of our people talking."

Bee held the blunt inches away from his lips. "What? Who?"

Teddy shook his head. "Don't know yet. I'll have the name in the morning."

The blunt had went out. Bee fired up the blunt again. He hit it twice and passed it to his brother. "So one of these niggas done got caught up and turned state?"

Teddy nodded. "Yep. Seems to be the story."

Bee rubbed his head with both hands. "Fuck! What they know?"

Teddy took three puffs and exhaled. "I don't know what he has or hasn't told, but I have shut down all movement fo' tonight."

The stress was on Bee. "Shit. Do Lil Will know?"

Teddy shook his head. "We can't depend on him to handle everything. We got this."

Bee hit the blunt so hard it made him choke. "Facts."

"Just lay low for a minute. I'll hit you up," Teddy said.

Bee nodded. "Damn, bruh. I just found out I'm about to be a father."

Teddy looked at him. "What? Get the fuck out of here! I'm

happy fo' you, bruh. More of a reason fo' you to lay low."

"Thanks. What up wit' Henry?" he asked Teddy.

Teddy shrugged his shoulders in a nonchalant way. "Who knows? I haven't seen or heard from my nigga in months."

Bee looked surprised. "Word?"

"Let me call him," Teddy said. He hit his line and it went straight to voicemail. Teddy hung up without leaving a message. "He ain't answering."

Bee looked concerned. "That ain't like Henry."

"I know, bruh. Maybe we should send somebody over there to check on that fool," Teddy said.

They sat around and finished smoking the blunt. Afterwards, Bee remembered he had told Trisha's fine ass he was coming through, so he told Teddy he would catch up with him later, and dipped.

He rolled up on the Westside beating the block down, listening to Scarface's "Scratch". It was nice outside, so most of the Westside niggas were on the basketball court balling. Bee even noticed Lil Nook standing on the sidelines. He was serving a fiend.

Bee pulled up in front of Trisha's spot and jumped out. She met him at the front door already down to her black Victoria's Secret. He stepped on through the door, kissing her, and kicked the door shut behind him.

"What took you so long, bae?" she asked while coming up out of the bra and panties.

Bee looked at her fine ass. "Money. It don't make itself."

Bee bent her over the edge of the sofa. He pulled down his pants and boxers and eased up inside of her from behind. She started to moan and thrust back hard against him. He complemented every thrust with an equally amount of force.

Bee fucked her long and hard from the back. There was something about looking at her fat juicy soft ass bounce that kept him pounding deep inside of her. She came back to back. But, when it was his time to cum, Bee pulled out and turned

Trisha around and she sucked him until he came in her mouth. She looked into his eyes while she continued to suck him dry and swallow every drop. Satisfied, he pulled up his boxers and pants and told her he had to go. Trisha told him she understood that he had to make his money and to stop by when he was available. He kissed her on the cheek and playfully slapped her on her ass before he left out of the house.

On his way to the car, Bee realized there was about to be some shit. Lil Nook was standing next to his car with his shirt off and arms folded across his chest.

"What up, my nigga?" Bee said as he walked up.

Lil Nook unfolded his arms. "Nigga, you know what time it is. Last time we hit, I was drunk. I ain't fucked up today, so let's try this shit again."

Fighting definitely wasn't on Bee's mind. He sighed. "My nigga, you got that li'l bit today. A nigga tired and his mind is on some more shit."

Lil Nook smirked. "I know I got it, fool. Learn to stay in your lane, bitch nigga."

Bee started laughing. Most people knew of his reputation. In the streets on the Southside, he was known as the knockout king. To other people in the public, he was a Golden Glove boxer.

Bee took off his jewelry and put it in his front right pocket. "Alright, my nigga. You just asked for this ass cutting."

Lil Nook ran up on Bee swinging. Bee weaved and bobbed his punches without putting much effort into it.

"Nigga, is that all you got?" Bee asked while dancing around light on his feet.

Bee weaved a right hook before throwing two quick jabs to Lil Nook's face. He was dazed from the jabs. He swung wildly trying to keep Bee off him, but it didn't work. Bee kept his guard up and rushed in, taking him out with a three piece snack; a left and right jab, then a left hook.

Lil Nook hit the concrete, unconscious. Bee looked around,

making sure nobody else was trying to get at him. When he saw it wasn't a hood beef against him, he jumped in his ride and left.

****

Henry was getting a little impatient with the fact that he had paid Nod to do a job that hadn't been done. He knew Mike was still breathing because the streets were always talking.

And when a nigga was making money like Mike made, a bitch would forever keep his name in her mouth. Frustrated, he called Nod to see what the holdup was.

The phone rang and rang. Finally, Nod answered. "What up?"

"Why ain't the nigga dead yet?" asked Henry.

"Some niggas take a li'l more time to kill than others. My work is official," Nod replied in a professional tone of voice.

Henry was not trying to hear the professional jargon. "Well, kill the nigga already."

Henry hung up. "Dammit. If you want something done, you got to do it yourself," he said to himself.

****

Nod was sitting in the parking lot of Wal-Mart. "Where the fuck this nigga at?" he thought out loud. Just as he was about to leave, he spotted him. He was dropping his little brother off at work. He smiled. "I got that ass now."

He waited. His adrenaline was pumping, thinking about the other fifty thousand he would collect after the job was done. When his mark pulled off, he eased into traffic behind him.

Damn, I love my job. Easy money, baby, he thought to himself. He pulled out the two chrome 40s and set them on the passenger seat. He was ready to get it over with.

Mike was on his way to check the trap house. As he drove, he had an ill feeling that something was up. He looked through the rearview mirror, and just as he thought, someone was tailing him. He took a detour just to confirm his suspicion, and when the unmarked car continued to follow him, he knew he wasn't tripping.

Thinking it was the feds, Mike floored the Benz, running every red light and stop sign. The Ford was right behind him. He realized it couldn't be the cops when the sirens didn't show.

He turned down a side street, jumped out, and hit the pavement running. Nod peeped as he hit the fence. "Damn, this nigga fast, but I got you, nigga, believe that," he said to himself.

Nod jumped out and ran behind him. "Nigga, ain't no need fo' running! I'm going to put some hot slugs in yo' ass tonight!"

They ran through backyards and on to different streets. Mike peeped a house with the back door open and ran in closing it fast as he ducked out of sight. Nod had lost sight of him.

"Damn, that nigga runs like a rabbit. Where did you go? Think. Think. Think," Nod thought out loud. As he was about to go left, a shot went off, hitting him in the shoulder.

"Fuck!" Nod ducked behind the nearest tree. Blood was soaking through his shirt. "Fuck nigga, you dead!"

"Nigga, who the fuck are you?" yelled Mike.

"I'm yo' grim reaper, bitch," Nod yelled back.

"Oh yeah? We'll see 'bout that!" yelled Mike. Mike eased the door open and aimed in the direction he had heard the voice.

What most people didn't know about Mike that he was an expert with a gun. He had learned how to break them down, clean them, put them back together and shoot any gun you put

Willie Slaughter

in his hands at the age of nine. He let two rounds off, hitting the tree Nod was posted behind.

"A'ight, my nigga. Let's keep this shit G! Your gun lying on the ground at my feet, so I know you know you fucked up," said Mike.

Nod breathed harshly. He knew he had picked the wrong job. He also knew this day would come, but damn, he didn't think it would be so soon.

Mike checked his clip. He had three rounds left. "I'm going to give yo' ass five seconds to do the right thing! 5! 4! 3! 2!"

"Hold up, my nigga!" Nod came from behind the tree with his hands up.

Mike looked at him, confused. "Who the fuck are you? Why you following me? You fed or something? Talk, nigga."

He didn't answer. His silence caused another bullet to strike him in the leg. Nod went down on one knee. "Fuck, man!"

"Oh, now your ass got a voice. Talk, nigga. I ain't got all night. The next one you getting to the dome," Mike threatened.

As he aimed at his head, Nod put his hands up. "Alright, my nigga. Put the gun down. I was paid to kill you."

Mike lowered his aim. "Really? By who? Henry?"

Nod nodded his head. "Yeah."

"How much?" Mike asked.

"Nigga put one hundred racks on your head, my nigga," he replied.

Mike whistled. "Dammit, man!" He laughed, thinking about the situation. "Look, nigga, it would be my loss if I put a slug in your face right now. I need you to do something fo' me."

Nod looked up at him. "Like what?

"Say I give you 250,000 to smoke his ass," Mike said.

Nod's eyes went wide. "Damn, nigga. You offering me that much after I just tried to bust your ass?"

Mike laughed. "Yeah, nigga. I advise you to give me an answer before I have a change of heart."

"No pressure. I'm in," said Nod.

Mike helped him to his feet. "Do the shit right. And you got three days."

"Consider it done, my nigga," replied Nod.

Mike shook hands with Nod. Looking into Nod's eyes, he didn't see a soul. Only a heartless killer.

Willie Slaughter

Chapter Thirteen

After Mark met up with Lil Will in Cali, they made their way to Texas. Three SUV's, fully-manned, waited on them at the airport.

"Good day, sir." One of the bodyguards opened the door.

They jumped in without responding. All three vehicles pulled out.

Lil Will knew it was going to be a long day and this meeting was the big break they needed. So he knew he had to be on point.

"Listen Mark, if all goes well, we'll be very rich after this day," Lil Will said. Mark's expression was serious. "I'm with you, fam."

"Good," said Lil Will.

Mark had been thinking about the situation with Monica and Erica. It wasn't too much to say about it since they were officially unsolved mysteries. But it was on his mind.

"Lil Will," he began to say, "was that shit really necessary with Monica and Erica? I mean, come on, fam, you act as if the bitch broke your heart or something. And with most of the shit we be out here doing, I know that ain't the case."

Lil Will looked at Mark with a straight face. "Mark, you my nigga and all, but do me and yourself a personal favor. Stay the fuck out of my personal business. Understood?"

Mark nodded. "All day, fam."

****

The head man was enjoying a meal at the estate when one of his guards walked in and said, "Sir, Lil Will is on his way."

He looked up from his meal and nodded. "Good. Anybody

Willie Slaughter

else arrived yet?"

"No sir. I'll keep you updated," the guard replied.

He smiled. "Thank you."

Upon being dismissed, the guard left the room and returned to his post near the front door. The head of the estate relaxed in his chair in deep thought. The day had come where he was ready to get out of the life. The seat would be passed.

There was a knock on the door. "Enter!"

Agent Wright walked in. "Sir."

Agent Wright was a good-looking, all business, and deeply-tanned Sicilian. She looked straight black at 5'7", petite with long flowing black hair. She was one amongst the many FBI agents on the drug lord's payroll.

He looked up at her with a straight face. "Sit down. I've been getting bad reports."

Agent Wright took a seat in one of the leather chairs. "Sir, my partner wants Lil Will off the streets."

"Any idea why?" he asked Agent Wright.

She shook her head. "No sir."

"Well, you need to find out, Agent Wright. There's too much at stake here. Lil Will can't be touched. He is the next me. Do you understand what I'm saying, Agent Wright?"

Agent Wright eyes widened. "But sir, he is hot."

He looked unconcerned with her explanation. "Make the heat go away."

She sighed. "I'll get on it right away, Sir."

His expression turned more serious. "Not next year, Agent Wright."

"Sir, I'll do everything in my power," she said in a definite tone of voice.

Hearing her reassuring answer, the smile returned to his face. "Thank you. Now let's have a drink while we wait on everyone to get here."

The head of the estate pushed the button underneath the desk. It wasn't a minute later that the butler appeared. "What

138

can I get you, sir?"

The head of the estate looked at Agent Wright. "What will you be drinking, my friend?"

"I will have a Scotch on the rocks," she said.

He turned his attention back to the butler. "Agent Wright here will be having a Scotch on the rocks. You already know what my preference is."

The butler nodded. "As you wish, sir. I shall return with your drinks shortly."

After the butler left, the head of the estate continued to explain to the agent the importance of making sure Lil Will stay in the clear. She expressed her understanding verbally, but deep down inside, she really didn't understand what would make him put a billion dollar operation in the hands of a street thug.

****

Ju-Ju was knocked out when Tee came in. Tee tapped him on the foot. "Aye nigga, wake up!"

Caught off guard, Ju-Ju jumped. "Man, what the fuck?"

Tee's facial expression was serious. "Bruh, I just got word yo' girl got killed."

His eyelids shot open. "Who? Monica?"

Tee looked at him sideways. "Yeah. Who else, fool?"

Ju-Ju got up. "What happened?"

Tee shook his head. "They say it was a car bomb. Two people dead. Damn, do you think Erica was with her?"

Ju-Ju punched the wall. "Fuck, nigga! Let's get back to Boston. This nigga gots to die."

They packed up and was heading out when Ju-Ju's phone rang. It was his brother. "Yo, bro. Talk to me."

"I got good news," his brother said.

"Spit it out," Ju-Ju demanded.

"Lil Will in Texas. We can go down there and twist his shit loose without anyone knowing," his brother informed him.

Ju-Ju became excited "Shit, let's do it."

"Meet me at the airport at eight o' clock," said his brother.

"I'll be there," Ju-Ju replied.

They hung up. Ju-Ju turned to his partner Tee, smiling. "Let's hurry up. We got to fly up to Bean Town to meet my brother at the airport at 8."

"I'm ready to go now," Tee replied.

They made their flight to Boston on time. They looked around for Ju-Ju's brother. Tee was on edge because he had to go to the bathroom. After walking around for the third time and not seeing him, Tee let it be known. "Damn, I got to piss."

Ju-Ju laughed. "Shit, don't feel bad. I been trying to hold off until I see this nigga, but fuck it. Let's hit the bathroom."

They grabbed their luggage and went to the restroom. The first person they saw inside pacing back and forth was his brother. Seeing Ju-Ju, he smirked and said, "I'm hoping you niggas are ready."

Tee ignored him, but Ju-Ju didn't. "Yeah. Just let a nigga piss in peace first."

He waited on them silently. After they washed their hands, he grabbed his brother by the arm. "Let's take a quick walk."

Ju-Ju snatched loose. "A'ight. Grab the bags, Tee."

They walked out into the waiting area to make sure they didn't miss their flight. Ju-Ju didn't know how his brother was ready to play it with Lil Will, so he said, "Listen, bruh, you might want to lock this nigga up, but I'm ready to body his ass."

His brother smiled. "So am I. The nigga killed my wife in the process of trying to get at me, so you got to know that I want this nigga's head on a pike."

Ju-Ju nodded. "Damn, bro. I didn't know. My condolences. So what's the move?"

"He's having a meeting with some very power people from

all over. They fly in once a year to discuss business. After the meeting, we'll follow him and off his ass," explained his brother.

Ju-Ju shrugged his shoulders. "I'm with it."

Ju-Ju's brother patted him on the shoulder. "That's what I wanted to hear. After we do this, I'm going to need you to lay low. I'll go back to work and throw a monkey wrench in the mix to cover our tracks."

They pounded each other up.

"Let's just get this shit over with," said Ju-Ju.

"Yeah, you right," his brother replied.

They boarded their flight. After takeoff, Ju-Ju went to the bathroom and made a call.

The person on the other end answered. "Talk. What's the move?"

"In the air, headed to Texas. I need that handled by the time I get back," said Ju-Ju.

"Say no more. I'll have my men on it," the guy replied.

"That's what's up. Go by the spots and collect the dues. Afterward, shut 'em down. It'll be too hot to move in a minute," cautioned Ju-Ju.

"Say no more," the man said.

****

Henry was riding down 10th when he spotted a familiar face. He knew he knew the nigga from back in the day, but he just couldn't put a name to the face. He pulled up on the curb and hopped out. "Say, my man, don't I know you?"

He eyed Henry closely. "Maybe. What ya need, young G?"

Henry walked up on him. "Nigga, ain't you T?"

"Yeah. Stop wasting my time, G," he said in a serious tone.

"I'm Henry. Henry Thomas's son," said Henry.

T started laughing. "Well I'll be damned."

They laughed and hugged.

Tony Taylor, a.k.a. T, was one of Henry's father's partners since way back when. He had put hot lead in several niggas and broads alike for playing with his money. Matter of fact, that's why T had caught a bid.

"Man, where you been?" asked Henry.

"Doing time for the past twenty-eight years," said T.

"About that. I found the nigga who did ya pops and rocked his ass to sleep," said Henry.

"Appreciate that, young G," T said.

"I did what I had to do," responded Henry.

T nodded. "That's right. Anyway, what's been going on with you, Lil Henry?"

Henry rubbed the back of his head. "A long story, man."

T laughed. "Shit, I got time."

Henry started walking back towards his car. "Come on. Get it."

T jumped in. Henry took him to the mall and bought him some clothes and shoes. Afterwards, he asked T where he wanted to eat at. He told him it didn't matter, so they stopped at a mom and pop like spot.

As they ate, Henry filled him in on the good and the bad. T whistled. "Dammit, Lil Henry. Shit been real fo you."

Henry chuckled. "Yeah. So where you staying at, OG?"

"Nowhere permanently. Bouncing around from bitch to bitch right now," said T.

Henry shook his head, laughing. "I got you, bruh. You can chill at my crib as long as you like."

"Thanks Lil Henry," said T.

"No problem," replied Henry.

"Lil Henry. Boy, I knew you would end up being a man like your pops. All business," T said.

Henry sighed, remembering his father. "Yeah, he is a true legend and I miss him."

T's expression turned serious. "If you need me, Henry,

don't hesitate to get at me."

"That's love, fam," Henry said as they got up to leave. As they exited the restaurant, his phone went off. He looked at the caller ID. It was Nod. "Nigga, it's about time," Henry said sarcastically.

"Yeah. Meet me with my money," Nod said, sounding all serious.

Henry frowned "Is the job finished?"

"Yeah. Bring my money. I'll be on the Eastside 21st and 18th. The old warehouse in an hour," he said.

Henry didn't like the shit he was saying. "A'ight." He hung up with a puzzled look on his face. Something wasn't right. Nod knew better than to get personal on the phone.

"What's up, Lil Henry? Is everything everything?" T asked, concerned.

He scratched his head. "Something ain't right."

"What?" asked T.

Henry was frustrated. "That problem I was telling you about supposed to be solved. But I got an itchy feeling 'bout the shit."

T put his thinking cap on. "Give me a quick rundown."

"The nigga just hit my line telling me to meet him on the Eastside," Henry explained.

"Say no more. Let's ride. Nigga, tell me you got handles," T said.

Henry laughed. "Every kind that's made."

T rubbed his hands together. "Let's pull up. Give me the goods about this nigga Nod."

"The nigga got a rep. Originally from Cali and a nineteen year army vet. Known for twisting shit up. We did good business once before," explained Henry.

T shrugged his shoulders. "Don't mean shit to me. I got something he don't."

"And what's that," asked Henry?

T looked at him and smiled. "Street smarts. Now let's see

143

what this fool talking 'bout."

As they got to the corner of 21st, T told him to let him out.

Henry was curious. "For what?"

T laughed. "He is waiting on you. Not me. If he makes a country break, I'll knock his ass off from the blindside."

Henry nodded, liking the idea. "Smart move."

"Yeah. You just be careful. Talk to the nigga until I get in position," said T.

Henry frowned. "How will I know?"

T shook his head. "You won't."

T hopped out and crept low and fast. Henry pulled off, headed to his destination. As he came to a stop, he picked up his phone and hit Nod on speed dial.

"Nigga, where you at?" Henry asked when he answered.

"On my way. 'Bout two minutes out," responded Nod.

"A'ight," said Henry and hung up the phone. Henry knew Nod better than he gave him credit for. He knew Nod was already there. He just was trying to see if he was alone.

Nod watched as the car pulled up at a creep. He could see Henry was looking from warehouse to warehouse. He hopped out and walked into the first warehouse. Nobody was there. He went in warehouse number two thinking and hoping T would come through in the clutch.

Henry turned on the light. Nobody there, but a few cars. "Damn," he thought out loud. He looked around, but not up, and that's where Nod was, on the roof watching him with his pistol already cocked.

Henry was getting impatient. He got on the phone and called him.

Nod answered with his Bluetooth. "Yeah, I'm here."

Henry looked around. "Good, let's get this over with."

"Where you at?" asked Nod.

"I'm in the second warehouse," said Henry.

Nod grinned. "Good." Nod hung up and crept down the stairs. "What up, my nigga? No. No. Don't do it. Hands up and

144

turn around."

Henry closed his eyes in disbelief. He had gotten caught slipping. "What's up with this shit? Nigga, you folding on a nigga for a hundred thousand, my nigga?"

Nod came in down the stairs. "A lot more money. It seems like someone wanted you dead a lot more and gave me more reasons to get the job done."

Henry shrugged. "Since I'm dead, at least give me a name?"

"If you must know, Mike," Nod replied.

Henry acted as if he was surprised. "I thought you offed him."

Nod laughed. "I damn near got offed. The nigga knows his craft."

Henry shook his head. He kept talking, thinking to buy some time for T to get in position. "Damn. Where is the loyalty in the game?"

Nod smirked. "Nigga, loyalty only got one color. And it's green. Well, nice knowing ya."

As Nod raised the gun, a shot came from behind him and he dropped dead. T had domed him, causing blood to splatter all over Henry.

Henry looked at the blood staining his shirt and pants. "What the fuck?!"

"Shhh... Let's get the hell out of here. I ain't tryin' to do another bid," T said at a whisper.

He walked on down the same stairs Nod had come down. He fished Nod's keys out of his pockets. "I'll take that nice new Jeep he was driving."

"Fine by me. Follow me to my spot. I'll let you in, but I got to go take care of my money business," said Henry.

"Sounds good to me," replied T.

Willie Slaughter

Chapter Fourteen

Inside the estate, the doorman welcomed the visitors into the meeting room. Inside was a ballroom-sized long table made out of black and grey swirled marble. The chairs were nicely carved oak padded with black leather.

"Have a seat. Mr. Cobb will be with you momentarily. Would you like something to drink?" asked the butler.

"No thanks," replied Lil Will. Lil Will looked around. He was so caught up in the moment, he didn't realize the man had entered the room.

"You like what you see?" asked the man who'd stepped into the waiting room.

Lil Will continued to look around. "It's nice"

The man watched him closely. "One day you will have your own."

Lil Will shook his head. "I'm good. It's too big for my taste."

The two men hugged. And then another came walking down the stairs into the room. Lil Will couldn't believe his eyes. They were twins.

The first of the twins he'd encountered laughed. "What's wrong, Lil Will? You look like you've seen a ghost."

Lil Will's facial expression was priceless. "That's why..."

"Yes, that's why nobody can put us in one place. Two heads and four eyes and ears," the twin who was walking down the stairs said.

Even Mark was awestruck.

The head laughed. "Don't look so surprised. We've been doing this forty plus years now. You two are the first to see us together under the same roof."

The head's twin looked at Lil Will and smiled. "Wow! My brother looks at you like a son and I can see why. Let's get down to business."

They walked down the hall to the other side of the estate.

They entered another ballroom-sized room with the same setting. Only difference was, people were seated waiting on them. The twins walked in and everybody stood until they reached the head of the table and sat down.

"Sit. Sit. You all are my guests," said the head.

Lil Will and Mark realized they were in the presence of the elite league. Judges, lawyers DA's, fed. You name it, it was at the table.

The head and his brother took a seat. "Everyone, I put this meeting together for a great cause: to let you all know I'm retiring." He looked at his brother. "Well, we are retiring, to be more specific."

Everyone gasped. One of the judges rose to his feet. "What? Why?"

"Well, you spend forty years handling the most complex business on the planet then tell me about it. No, but seriously. It's my time. I've given my blessing to the one who shall be taking my place.

He knows the game in and out. And he's been bringing great fortune to this business," said the head.

The doorman walked in. "Sir, Mr. Cobb, may I have a word with you?"

He knew something wasn't right. As his chief of security left the room, he called Lil Will up to him.

"Yes? What is going on?" asked Lil Will.

"I think we have a big problem," he replied.

Lil Will nodded. "Understood."

Lil Will nodded to Mark and they left the room. Out in the hallway, they stopped. "What's up?" asked Mark.

Lil Will rubbed his head. "Something is going on and he wants us to look into it." Mark pulled out his twin 9 mm with extended clips. "Let's do it."

The head of the estate and the guest left out through a secret passage. Lil Will and Mark had gone directly to the security room where Mr. Cobb was viewing the footage.

"Mr. Cobb, what's the problem?" asked Mark. He moved to the side.

"See for yourself."

On the security camera screen, three masked men crept around the place, leaving bodies in their path. Mark looked a little closer. There was something familiar about the way one of the gunmen moved.

"I'll be damned," said Mark.

Mr. Cobb looked at him surprisingly. "What? You know them?"

Mark nodded and pointed at the security cameras screen. "That walk. The third guy. That's the exact way that nigga Ju-Ju walks. That means one of the other two must be his brother, Agent Scott. We got this, Mr. Cobb."

Mr. Cobb waved him off. "Nonsense. My man will help you."

The doorman walked in with a pump and a 9mm.

Mark looked surprised. "Wait a minute. Ain't he the doorman?"

Mr. Cobb laughed and patted Mark on the shoulder. "That's just one of his many talents, Mark. But no. he's my personal bodyguard."

Lil Will chuckled while cocking his gun. "Let's handle this situation. Mark, go 'round back. I'll go up on the roof."

The doorman looked his weapons over. "I'll go with Mark." The doorman shouldered the pump and cocked the 9mm.

Lil Will checked his clip. "Let's end this shit."

Ju-Ju, his brother and partner Tee posted up on the side of the house.

"Man, this shit seems too easy. You sho' they ain't waiting on us?" asked Tee, feeling uneasy about the whole situation.

Agent Scott peeped around the corner of the house. "I doubt it. Remember, they came for a meeting."

Tee frowned, really not believing shit Scott said. "Then

where the cars? I don't see shit."

Scott became irritated with Tee. "Shut the fuck up and move. It's too late to turn back now"

Just as Ju-Ju moved to the corner of the house, bullets started flying his way. He damn near caught one in the face.

"Fuck!" Ju-Ju yelled as he ducked back around the house for a second. "Looks like you know what the fuck you were talking about, Scott."

He returned fire. His brother was right there with him. Scott tried to get a better shot off at the gunners and slipped on Mark and the doorman who came up from behind.

"Watch out!" Tee jumped in the line of fire and caught every slug that was meant for Ju-Ju and his brother. His warning gave Scott just enough time to escape through the door he was next to. Ju-Ju, on the other hand, didn't. Mark didn't shoot to kill him, but he put one in his leg.

Mark and the doorman kept their guns aimed at Ju-Ju. Mark stepped up near him. "Ju-Ju, it's over with for you. Drop the gun. Slowly."

"Fuck you, nigga!" Ju-Ju spent fast, but not fast enough. The doorman laid him down with two shots to the head.

He reloaded the 9 mm and the pump. "Two down. One to go."

Lil Will came running. He reached them just as Mark unmasked the two dead bodies. "Well, look at these two bitches."

Lil Will looked at the faces of Ju-Ju and Tee. "Dead bitches. Just like their bitches. Come on, man. Let's go."

They walked back inside. Mr. Cobb met them in the hallway. "Great job. No need to worry about the other man. I watched him leave the compound in a hurry. Besides, you can consider him dead already."

Mr. Cobb smiled. "Right this way. The meeting is ready to be continued."

They walked down the long hallway making small talk. When they entered the room, everybody stood to their feet.

The head of the estate clapped in response to how fast they handled the situation. "Everyone, meet your new head of this table. Lil Will, it's your time, my son."

Everybody raised their glasses in salute to their new leader. Lil Will picked up a glass of wine himself and raised it, saluting everyone back.

"I would like to thank you for your support and I will see to it that business stays business," promised Lil Will.

The head of the estate motioned for Lil Will to join him at the head of the table. "If there are any questions or concerns, please feel free to make them known. I'm sure Lil Will does not mind listening to the concerns of people who will have his best interest in life. Besides, let's keep business being business."

One of the judges stood up. He was an old, balding, gray-headed Caucasian who looked very familiar to Lil Will. "I have been of great service to you, sir."

The head of the estate nodded. "That you have, Mr. Sampson. And I hope to continue with our working business relationship."

Sampson scratched his balding head. "With all due respect, sir, I, for one, am not sure if he will be able to handle this position you have bestowed upon him. He is a street thug, a hoodlum. I honestly think we are going to spend more money and time having to deal with his preexisting problems than we are getting paid."

Lil Will held his right hand up. "If I may, Mr. Sampson?"

"Go ahead," the judge replied.

Lil Will finished off his drink and set the glass on the table. "You have every right to feel like you do. To be honest with you, I don't really give a fuck how you feel. You don't put money in my account. I am the one who makes sure you are paid that nice salary you send your wife, children, and grandchildren on vacations with. If you want to stop being able to do that, then I suggest you get the fuck on."

The judge looked at Lil Will with a look of hatred. He then turned his attention to the head of the estate. "Do you see what I mean? The man is a menace to society. No respect for business."

The head of the estate shook his head. He already knew Judge Sampson was going to be a problem for Lil Will. That left him with only one decision to make concerning the judge.

"Judge Sampson, are you saying that you want out of this business due to the fact that Lil Will is heading it now?"

He downed his glass of wine and nodded. "You have said it, sir."

"So, you don't trust my judgment Mr. Sampson," asked the head?

The judge shook his head. "Not on this one, sir. It has been a pleasure working with you; however, I will not jeopardize my family or myself by working with a street thug, who knows nothing about how this business really works."

The head of the estate nodded. "I - we - appreciate your honesty and I appreciate all you have done for me and this business, Mr. Sampson." He looked over at his chief of security. "Mr. Cobb, would you be so kind to escort Judge Sampson here to a more suitable place until we are done with this meeting?"

"Yes, sir." The chief of security walked over to the judge and stood beside him. "Please follow me, sir."

Judge Sampson walked out of the room with Mr. Cobb.

The head of the estate had asked that a laptop be brought into the room. The butler had brought it in and set it up on the table in a position where everyone was able to see the screen. They could see Judge Sampson being escorted somewhere off of the premises.

As they watched the judge walking in front of the chief of security, the unexpected happened. Mr. Cobb pulled out a concealed handgun that had a silencer on it. He aimed directly at the back of the judge's head and squeezed the trigger.

"As I said beforehand," the head began saying, "let's keep business being business. No one likes an unhealthy business relationship. Let Sampson be a reminder to you all what happens to people who decide they know what is best for business. A business that none of you have to run, but continue to get paid for your great services in making sure everything runs smoothly."

Nobody said a word. Even Lil Will was quiet, in deep thought. He knew the business had its sacrifices and bloodshed when necessary, but now he was given to understand that nobody was exempt from dying when it came down to it. *Damn, I have a lot to learn about this shit*, he thought to himself.

After the little show was over, the butler closed the laptop and took it off the table. The head of the estate excused himself, pulling Lil Will out of the room and off to the side in the hallway. "Lil Will, you have a lot of learning to do. Those people in there are your lifeline. You know what that means?"

Lil Will nodded. "Yes sir. Keep them paid and happy, and they will keep me safe and sound."

The head of the estate shook his head and sighed. "Lil Will, that is only a small portion of this business. You got to know what to say more than you do when. You don't need to bite off the hands of the people who holds the offices that can ruin your life."

Understanding what he was saying to him, Lil Will nodded. "I appreciate the talk. Hopefully, you will continue to be an advisor to me until I get this down to a science."

The head of the estate patted him on the shoulder. "Just when I thought you would never ask. Of course, I will assist you where I see fit. This business isn't that hard to run. It pretty much runs itself. All you need to concern yourself with is directing the flow of the intake and out take of money and product."

Lil Will nodded. The head of the estate, seeing that he understood, walked back into the meeting room with Lil Will following in his footsteps. They took their seats. But this time, Lil Will sat at the head of the table.

Chapter Fifteen

Agent Scott had made it back to Boston. He had slept during the flight so he was rested and ready to go to work. The airport was having a busy day, so the luggage department was moving slowly. Since he had to use the bathroom, he did not mind. He walked into the restroom.

"Shit, I got to piss," he thought out loud. He closed his eyes as he relieved himself at the urinal.

The door opened behind him, but he didn't pay the person any attention, which was a fatal mistake. He didn't hear the gunshots, but he felt the heat as the bullets pierced him through the back of the head.

The man, dressed in the blue pinstripe Armani suit and casual low cut Timberland's, unscrewed the silencer off the gun and placed it in a case. He took out his phone and made a call.

"Hello?" the man on the other end of the line said as he answered his phone.

The man in the Armani suit closed the case and wiped down while he talked on the phone with his employer. "Business handled."

"We appreciate your service, Agent Dunlap. The money is being transferred to your account now," said the employer.

"Thank you," he replied.

He hung up and walked out of the bathroom, leaving the dead man slumped face down in the in the urinal.

The employer pressed the end call icon on the phone. He leaned back in his chair, thinking to himself what a hell of a day it had been. But he knew it wasn't as bad as the coming days have the potential to be. With that thought, he picked up his phone and made an important call.

"Hello?" the female answered.

"Hi my friend." He started saying. "I hope you're really up to the task of keeping our mutual friend on the straight and narrow."

The woman laughed. "No pressure Demetri. I got him."

"Great Machumu. I always could count on you to do what's best for business." Demetri replied.

Before she could respond, Demetri ended the call. He kicked his feet up on the desk and interlocked his fingers behind his head, considering the many possibilities of the future.

To Be Continued...
Slaughter Gang 2
Coming Soon

Submission Guideline

Submit the first three chapters of your completed manuscript to ldpsubmissions@gmail.com, subject line: Your book's title. The manuscript must be in a .doc file and sent as an attachment. Document should be in Times New Roman, double spaced and in size 12 font. Also, provide your synopsis and full contact information. If sending multiple submissions, they must each be in a separate email.

Have a story but no way to send it electronically? You can still submit to LDP/Ca$h Presents. Send in the first three chapters, written or typed, of your completed manuscript to:

LDP: Submissions Dept
Po Box 870494
Mesquite, Tx 75187

DO NOT send original manuscript. Must be a duplicate.

Provide your synopsis and a cover letter containing your full contact information.

Thanks for considering LDP and Ca$h Presents.

Coming Soon from Lock Down Publications/Ca$h Presents

BOW DOWN TO MY GANGSTA

By **Ca$h**

TORN BETWEEN TWO

By **Coffee**

BLOOD STAINS OF A SHOTTA **III**

By **Jamaica**

STEADY MOBBIN **III**

By **Marcellus Allen**

BLOOD OF A BOSS **VI**

By **Askari**

LOYAL TO THE GAME **IV**

LIFE OF SIN III

By **T.J. & Jelissa**

A DOPEBOY'S PRAYER **II**

By **Eddie "Wolf" Lee**

IF LOVING YOU IS WRONG... **III**

LOVE ME EVEN WHEN IT HURTS **III**

By **Jelissa**

TRUE SAVAGE **VII**

By **Chris Green**

BLAST FOR ME **III**

DUFFLE BAG CARTEL III

By **Ghost**

ADDICTIED TO THE DRAMA **III**

By **Jamila Mathis**

A HUSTLER'S DECEIT 3

Slaughter Gang

KILL ZONE **II**

BAE BELONGS TO ME III

SOUL OF A MONSTER

By **Aryanna**

THE COST OF LOYALTY **III**

By **Kweli**

SHE FELL IN LOVE WITH A REAL ONE **II**

By **Tamara Butler**

RENEGADE BOYS **III**

By **Meesha**

CORRUPTED BY A GANGSTA **IV**

By **Destiny Skai**

A GANGSTER'S SYN II

By **J-Blunt**

KING OF NEW YORK V

RISE TO POWER III

COKE KINGS II

By **T.J. Edwards**

GORILLAZ IN THE BAY III

De'Kari

THE STREETS ARE CALLING II

Duquie Wilson

KINGPIN KILLAZ IV

STREET KINGS 2

PAID IN BLOOD 2

Hood Rich

SINS OF A HUSTLA II

ASAD

TRIGGADALE II

Willie Slaughter

Elijah R. Freeman
MARRIED TO A BOSS III
By Destiny Skai & Chris Green
KINGS OF THE GAME III
Playa Ray
SLAUGHTER GANG II
By Willie Slaughter

<u>Available Now</u>
<u>RESTRAINING ORDER</u> **I & II**
By **CA$H & Coffee**
<u>LOVE KNOWS NO BOUNDARIES</u> **I II & III**
By **Coffee**
<u>RAISED AS A GOON I, II, III & IV</u>
<u>BRED BY THE SLUMS I, II, III</u>
<u>BLAST FOR ME I & II</u>
<u>ROTTEN TO THE CORE I III</u>
<u>A BRONX TALE I, II, III</u>
<u>DUFFEL BAG CARTEL I II</u>
By **Ghost**
<u>LAY IT DOWN</u> **I & II**
<u>LAST OF A DYING BREED</u>
<u>BLOOD STAINS OF A SHOTTA I & II</u>
By **Jamaica**
<u>LOYAL TO THE GAME</u>
<u>LOYAL TO THE GAME II</u>
<u>LOYAL TO THE GAME III</u>
<u>LIFE OF SIN I, II</u>

Slaughter Gang

By **TJ & Jelissa**

BLOODY COMMAS I & II

SKI MASK CARTEL I II & III

KING OF NEW YORK I II,III IV

RISE TO POWER I II

COKE KINGS

By **T.J. Edwards**

IF LOVING HIM IS WRONG...I & II

LOVE ME EVEN WHEN IT HURTS I II

By **Jelissa**

WHEN THE STREETS CLAP BACK I & II III

By **Jibril Williams**

A DISTINGUISHED THUG STOLE MY HEART I II & III

LOVE SHOULDN'T HURT I II III IV

RENEGADE BOYS I & II

By **Meesha**

A GANGSTER'S CODE I &, II III

A GANGSTER'S SYN

By J-Blunt

PUSH IT TO THE LIMIT

By **Bre' Hayes**

BLOOD OF A BOSS **I, II, III, IV, V**

By **Askari**

THE STREETS BLEED MURDER **I, II & III**

THE HEART OF A GANGSTA I II& III

By **Jerry Jackson**

CUM FOR ME

CUM FOR ME 2

CUM FOR ME 3

Willie Slaughter

Slaughter Gang

TRUE SAVAGE **V**

TRUE SAVAGE **VI**

By **Chris Green**

A DOPEBOY'S PRAYER

By **Eddie "Wolf" Lee**

THE KING CARTEL **I, II & III**

By **Frank Gresham**

THESE NIGGAS AIN'T LOYAL **I, II & III**

By **Nikki Tee**

GANGSTA SHYT **I II &III**

By **CATO**

THE ULTIMATE BETRAYAL

By **Phoenix**

BOSS'N UP **I , II & III**

By **Royal Nicole**

I LOVE YOU TO DEATH

By Destiny J

I RIDE FOR MY HITTA

I STILL RIDE FOR MY HITTA

By **Misty Holt**

LOVE & CHASIN' PAPER

By **Qay Crockett**

TO DIE IN VAIN

SINS OF A HUSTLA

By **ASAD**

BROOKLYN HUSTLAZ

By **Boogsy Morina**

BROOKLYN ON LOCK I & II

By **Sonovia**

Willie Slaughter

GANGSTA CITY
By **Teddy Duke**
A DRUG KING AND HIS DIAMOND I & II III
A DOPEMAN'S RICHES
HER MAN, MINE'S TOO I, II
CASH MONEY HO'S
By Nicole Goosby
TRAPHOUSE KING **I II & III**
KINGPIN KILLAZ I II III
STREET KINGS
PAID IN BLOOD
By **Hood Rich**
LIPSTICK KILLAH **I, II, III**
CRIME OF PASSION I & II
By **Mimi**
STEADY MOBBN' **I, II, III**
By **Marcellus Allen**
WHO SHOT YA **I, II, III**
Renta
GORILLAZ IN THE BAY **I II**
DE'KARI
TRIGGADALE
Elijah R. Freeman
GOD BLESS THE TRAPPERS I, II, III
THESE SCANDALOUS STREETS I, II, III
FEAR MY GANGSTA I, II, III
THESE STREETS DON'T LOVE NOBODY I, II
BURY ME A G I, II, III, IV, V
A GANGSTA'S EMPIRE I, II, III

164

Slaughter Gang

Tranay Adams
THE STREETS ARE CALLING

Duquie Wilson
MARRIED TO A BOSS... I II

By Destiny Skai & Chris Green
KINGS OF THE GAME I II

Playa Ray
SLAUGHTER GANG II

By Willie Slaughter

Willie Slaughter

BOOKS BY LDP'S CEO, CA$H

TRUST IN NO MAN

TRUST IN NO MAN 2

TRUST IN NO MAN 3

BONDED BY BLOOD

SHORTY GOT A THUG

THUGS CRY

THUGS CRY 2

THUGS CRY 3

TRUST NO BITCH

TRUST NO BITCH 2

TRUST NO BITCH 3

TIL MY CASKET DROPS

RESTRAINING ORDER

RESTRAINING ORDER 2

IN LOVE WITH A CONVICT

Coming Soon
BONDED BY BLOOD 2
BOW DOWN TO MY GANGSTA

www.ingramcontent.com/pod-product-compliance
Lightning Source LLC
Chambersburg PA
CBHW070838280626
47161CB00015B/1702